This book will nourish your soul, making you both laugh and cry! Heidi is an inspiring author with a fresh perspective, who meets you right where you are in life. Written with humor and sincerity, you'll look forward to reading every word!

—April Henry

Someone who understands what you're going through, has made it through themselves, and can point you to Christ is a rare find. Heidi takes the everyday moments of life and engages in the practice of always looking for God. After reading a few stories, you'll be encouraged to start the same practice of allowing God to use the mundane and difficult moments of your day to draw closer to Him.

—Linde Miller

Heidi has a unique gift of seeing God's profoundness in the ordinary, and she challenges me to do the same. She writes how my brain feels! I highly recommend this book!

—Faith Rice

Completely relatable! The stories in this book are so down to earth, addressing daily struggles and providing simple solutions that align with scripture. Truly an enjoyable read!

—Danielle Beard

Personable, relatable, and so well written! The connection between the raw vulnerability of real life and the Word of God is refreshing and uplifting. A must-read for mothers and wives who desire to grow closer to the Lord.

Leah Hockenberry

COFFEE TASTES BETTER in a QUIET HOUSE

lessons learned
from a perfectly
ordinary life

Heidi Poe

Cover & interior design by Typewriter Creative Co.

Scripture quotations marked (NIV) are taken from the Holy Bible, New International Version®, NIV®. Copyright © 1973, 1978, 1984, 2011 by Biblica, Inc.™ Used by permission of Zondervan. All rights reserved worldwide. www.zondervan.comThe "NIV" and "New International Version" are trademarks registered in the United States Patent and Trademark Office by Biblica, Inc.™

ISBN 979-8-9914446-0-6 (Paperback)
ISBN 979-8-9914446-1-3 (eBook)

Table of Contents

But first, let me explain...

I live an ordinary life.

I am a wife of over twenty-five years to my wonderful husband, who is incredibly handsome and hard-working. He is my rock and I am so blessed to be his wife. I am a mother to our two amazing daughters, who are now grown, despite my futile efforts to make time slow down. They are a joy to all who know them and I am so glad I can now count them as friends. But above all, I am a daughter of the Most-High God, my Lord and Savior Jesus Christ. I am imperfect, but saved by grace. Thank you, Lord!

I am honored to be the gatekeeper of our home. I plant and tend a garden (I love to feel the dirt between my fingers), bake sourdough bread (yes, I'm one of those), cook and clean, and do all things related to keeping our home running. It's not always smooth, but I keep it running, nonetheless!

I enjoy reading good books (the kind you just can't put down and stay up late into the night reading), writing lots of words (that sometimes make sense), and singing songs of praise, and other things (I am a big fan of Classic Country and often sing it way too loudly)! I like to crochet, although I am by no means an expert. But I can make a dishcloth like nobody's business! I adore all things Autumn: Changing colors, falling leaves, cooler temperatures, and apples (Honeycrisp are the best). I do not enjoy Summer. It is just too hot. In fact, Summer and I are sworn enemies. Fall is my one true love.

I like to spend time with my family, playing cards and board games. I must confess, I am not always a good sport. I have a bit of a competitive streak. In fact, I have flipped a game board or two in my day. Just ask my husband (sorry, Honey)! I love nature, and the beautiful mountains where we live, and spending lots of time outdoors (but not in the summer).

Some of my favorite things are chocolate and peanut butter (together or separately), the smell of freshly brewed coffee, and the first snowfall of the season. My favorite television show of all time is *The Andy Griffith Show*. The black and white episodes are the best. I quote the show on an almost daily basis. Just ask my husband (sorry, Honey)!

I was raised in the church and came to know Jesus at an early age (five years old, to the best of my recollection). I have been a Christian nearly all my life. I love the Lord and desire to serve Him and follow where He leads me. But I am far from perfect. I sin and struggle, but I try my best. I worry too much and sometimes say words I should not say. Just ask my husband (sorry, Honey)!

I live a very normal life, and have mostly stayed on the straight and narrow path, thank the Lord. I do not have a fascinating testimony. No defining hit rock bottom, come to Jesus moment, for which I am thankful. But honestly, because of this, I sometimes feel I have nothing to offer. I do not have a grand testimony or a heart-wrenching conversion story. (I need to add a side note here. If God has pulled you out of the pit, and you have a 'hit rock bottom" story, thank you for giving your life to the Lord. And thank you for sharing your testimony! God is so gracious and loving and is able to bring beauty from ashes)! But that is not my story. My story is ordinary.

For much of my life, I have felt that my ordinary story is not worth sharing. That it has no value. Or purpose. Because how can I encourage others without a grand story? But at some point, I realized I do not have to be like Billy Graham (or some other famous evangelist) to serve the Lord. I don't have to be a pastor, or best-selling author, or hold a degree in theology.

Maybe it's the wisdom that comes with age (and the inevitable gray hairs). Or maybe it's just a deeper connection with the Lord, which I'm confident is His doing and not mine! But I have realized that God can work through the ordinary. He shows up in the everyday. He teaches me through normal circumstances (like grocery shopping, making dinner and taking the dog for a walk). He reveals things to me about myself. Things I need to work on. And things I need to change. Honestly, I don't always like this! Change is hard. And I am stubborn. But God meets me where I am. In my average, regular, normal, everyday life.

As it turns out, ordinary is my testimony. And God wants me to share it. To use it to encourage others. It is not fancy, or grand, or awe-inspiring. But it is my life. And ordinary can be beautiful. In fact, it is extraordinary.

All that to say this book is a collection of stories from my normal, average, ordinary life and the extraordinary things God has taught me along the way. So, grab a cup of coffee (or your beverage of choice), settle in, and join me on a walk through my perfectly ordinary life.

ONE

Martha's Recipe for Tuna Casserole

I started the day with good intentions. I was going to write. Maybe not a lot, but some. Definitely for an hour. Or two. Several pages. Maybe ten pages. Ten sounded like a good number. There were other things on my to-do list, as well. Laundry. There was always laundry. I also needed to work on making some Christmas presents. I was crocheting cute little baskets that would be soaked in starch then left upside down to dry on mason jars. They were going to be adorable! And speaking of Christmas gifts, I had to do some online shopping. Three weeks until Christmas and I was not prepared.

What else was on my list? I wanted to read my Bible. Plus, there was a book I had started reading last month about how to be a good wife. Except, I didn't know where it was. I hadn't seen it in two weeks. I wasn't too worried, though. I just thought maybe I didn't need to read it anymore. Maybe this was God's way of telling me I was doing an awesome job as a wife and I didn't need any more help. But then I saw that book peeking out from under the edge of the couch. Staring at me. Taunting me. Saying, "Girl, please. You are not all that." I confess I was tempted to shove that book back under the couch with my big toe and pretend I didn't see it. But then I thought, *What can it hurt? I guess I could always use a little improvement. Even if I am rocking this wife thing.* So, I rescued the book from its hiding place and added it to my to-do list.

And then there was the email. I wanted to track the status of several packages I was expecting. I also needed to vacuum the living room rug. It was covered with dog hair, a piece of smushed popcorn, a few stray pine needles that had fallen off the Christmas tree, and a long piece of red string with a clump of fuzz at the end, all scattered across the floor.

Realistically, I knew I wouldn't complete every task on my list—but I was happy to cross off as many items as I could. I got started right after breakfast. With a nap. Hey, I was tired. I had already been up for three hours. Plus, I hadn't slept well the night before. So, I took a nap. Not a long one. Only twenty minutes. But it was nice just the same. With nap time behind me, I was refreshed and ready to tackle my list. But what to do first? I chose online Christmas shopping. There was no method to my madness. I just felt like shopping. Online, of course. I am not a "go to the mall and shop-til-you-drop" kind of girl. Public places are too people-y. So, I spent the next forty-five minutes, give or take an hour, searching for the perfect hoodie for my fifteen-year-old daughter. I knew the style she wanted. And the color. And the size. But for the life of me, I could not find one! On one site I found the right color, in a double XL. Nope, not the right size. She wore a medium. On another site I found a medium, but it was not the right color. And so it went for forty-five minutes, give or take an hour. I lost track of time, until I finally just gave up. On to the next task!

I had been working on laundry all morning. I threw another load into the washing machine and headed back to the living room, intending to get to my Bible reading. Or my writing. But that red fuzz on the floor was driving me nuts! So, I vacuumed the rug. Which scared the dog. Which prompted her to scratch at the back door. Which meant she needed to go out. So, I put on my boots and took her outside. The goats saw me and began screaming for attention. So, I gave them a treat and spent a few minutes with them. Or thirty. They are so cute and fluffy I can't resist their sweet little faces. But I had things to do, so back into the house I went.

I checked the laundry and a load was ready to be folded. Okay, now it was time to get down to business. I opened my Bible to the book of James (one of my favorites) and read the first chapter. Good stuff. Then I opened that dusty marriage book and read about yielding to my husband. Turns out there was a reason I had found that book today. Message received. Now to finally move on to my writing! I had just picked up my pen when my husband walked into the house for his lunch break. I asked him about his morning and we began chatting, which completely derailed my train of thought. Looks like I wasn't going to get any writing done today. So, why not have lunch? I was hungry, anyway. But I could multitask. I ate my spinach quesadilla while having a chat with my husband. Time well spent. He headed back to work and I folded another load of laundry.

What else was on my to-do list? Oh yeah, crochet baskets. I found some pretty blue yarn and started a new basket. I didn't get very far, though. The dog needed to go out again. This day was not going as planned. I was getting nowhere. What had I been doing for the last seven hours? It felt like I had been doing so many things but was getting nothing done. I needed another nap! A real one this time. So, I laid down on the couch and proceeded to watch an entire episode of The Andy Griffith Show. The Pickle Story. It's my favorite! And then I took a nap.

I promise you, not all of my days are so scattered and unproductive. There are days when I am so busy I dream of having an unproductive day! There are days when I'm on top of my game.

When I'm rocking it like a boss! Okay, those days don't happen very often. But there are many days when I act like a boss. Or maybe I'm just bossy. But whatever. You get the idea. Today I was not the boss of anything. Except nap time. I totally rocked that!

Today I was a mess. I was scattered and distracted. I had put too many things on my to-do list. I should have chosen just one thing. The most important thing. Today I should have been Mary. Do you remember the Bible story of Mary and Martha? Jesus came to town and Martha invited him into her home. Her sister, Mary, plopped herself down at the feet of Jesus so she could listen to what he had to say. But Martha was too busy. She had too many things to do. She was probably in the kitchen, frantically searching through the pantry, trying to throw together a last-minute meal. What do you serve the Son of God, anyway? Does he eat leftovers?

I can relate to Martha. And if I'm being totally honest, the story of Mary and Martha has always rubbed me the wrong way. Maybe it's because I see myself in this story. I am a doer. A planner. A "let's get things done" kind of girl. I am always the one behind the scenes, in the kitchen, washing those dishes. Or making an extra pan of fudge brownies, just in case. If there is a task that needs to be done, I like to do it. Not because I love washing dishes, but because I want to check it off my list. I can't relax knowing there is work that needs to be done.

I can imagine Martha's frustration with her sister. I mean, really, if Mary would have just offered to help Martha, the work would have been done in half the time, and maybe Martha could have sat at the feet of Jesus, too! Why should Martha have to do all the work? The truth is, Martha chose to do the work. She chose *not* to spend time with Jesus. Can you imagine? Think about it. Jesus, the Son of God, the King of Kings, came into Martha's house and she walked away. Into the kitchen. To make a tuna casserole. Her priorities were way off!

We read in Luke 10:40–42, "But Martha was distracted by all the preparations that had to be made. She came to him and asked, 'Lord, don't you care that my sister has left me to do the work by myself? Tell her to help me!'

'Martha, Martha,' the Lord answered, 'you are worried and upset about many things, but only one thing is needed. Mary has chosen what is better, and it will not be taken away from her.'" (NIV)

Did you catch that? First of all, wow was Martha gutsy! She literally marched straight up to Jesus and told him to make Mary help her! Sounds like she was in a mood. I can relate. But verse 40 says Martha was distracted. She had taken her focus off of Jesus. And that is what I did today. I filled up my day with stuff. I flitted from one thing to another. And I got nothing accomplished. I should have started my to-do list at the feet of Jesus, not searching for an olive green, size medium hoodie.

Yes, there will always be chores and responsibilities and laundry. And that's okay. As long as I remember that God is always my number one, most important priority! And if I remember that, everything else will fall into place.

I think I'll take another peek under the couch. God just might have another message for me.

PRAYER:

God, spending time in your presence is such
a joy! Thank you for giving me opportunities to sit
at your feet. Help me to always choose you!

Two

I'm Blaming My Hormones

I had a meltdown today. A full-blown temper tantrum. A yelling fit. It was as if my lips just took over. Like my mouth detached from my body to preserve itself so my brain wouldn't shut it down. Words were tumbling out of my mouth faster than my brain could form them. Like water cascading over Niagara Falls. Or a chubby kid rolling down a hill. Or Clark Griswold on a metal saucer flying down a snowy hill into the Wal-Mart parking lot in "Christmas Vacation."

I am claiming temporary insanity. I mean, I couldn't have been sane, right? A rational person doesn't lose her temper so quickly. A calm person doesn't explode like a baking soda volcano in a sixth-grade science fair. But I did! Like Mt. Vesuvius. Spewing lava and ash and whatever else comes out of a volcano. (I have no idea. I did not win that science fair.)

I think for times like these, there should be a pause button. Or rewind. Or some other fancy way of stopping myself. Because I certainly felt powerless to stop it on my own. I knew I needed to shut up, I just couldn't seem to make myself do it! And my poor husband, God bless him, couldn't have stopped me if he'd tried! He is a great man. He's a listener and a fixer. But he is not a stopper!

Oh, there have been times when he has tried to stop the overflow of my mouth. But somehow, for some strange reason, that only makes my words flow more. Like he's turning up the faucet or opening the flood gates. And I am not blaming him. It is not his fault. He tries, bless him!

In all honesty, I know the blame and responsibility lie with me. After all, it's my brain, my voice, my lips moving a mile a minute. In that moment when it seems I've lost control, I've really stolen it. From God. He is the captain of my ship. And when I veer off course—or in this case, when my mouth turns into Class V white-water rapids—it means that I've taken control, or really *stolen* control, from God. It means in that moment I am not allowing God to steer my words, my thoughts, or my mouth. And where does that lead me? Over Niagara Falls in a barrel. Every. Single. Time. It causes hurt to everyone who is close enough to hear my words, whoever is in the "splash zone." It causes pain to that poor soul being drenched by my barrage. It causes damage to my heart. And I think it hurts God, too.

So, what do I do? How do I stop my mouth? I could carry around a sandbag and shove it into my mouth when the words start to overflow. I mean, that's what they do when there's a hurricane a-coming, right? Staunch the flow (or overflow) of the water (or words, as the case may be). But honestly, I don't do sand. It's itchy and it gets in my toenails. No, a sandbag would not work for me.

But prayer! Asking the good Lord to help me shut my mouth. Like he did to those lions so they couldn't eat Daniel. Daniel 6:22 says, "My God sent his angel, and he shut the mouths of the lions. They have not hurt me, because I was found innocent in his sight. Nor have I ever done any wrong before you, Your Majesty." And in Matthew 21:22, Jesus says "If you believe, you will receive whatever you ask for in prayer."

So, I will pray. I'll ask the Lord to supernaturally close my mouth. Or give me five-minute laryngitis. (That's a thing, right?) Or maybe I should ask for patience, self-control. A loving heart. You know, all that good stuff. And maybe, just maybe, God will give me the strength to take control of my own mouth, my own heart. So maybe, just maybe, I can't blame my epic outburst on temporary insanity. Maybe, just maybe, I have to claim responsibility.

Or I can just blame it on hormones. That's legit, right? Lord, have mercy!

PRAYER:

Lord, words are powerful. They can encourage or cause harm. Help me to choose my words wisely and keep a tight rein on my tongue. I want to honor you with every word I speak.

THREE

Seek and Ye Shall Find, Just Be Sure to Look in the Right Place

My husband is a hunter. He loves spending time in the woods. He loves to hunt deer, especially in archery season. But he loves to take our daughters hunting more than anything. From the time our girls were young, Daddy would take them for walks in the woods. He taught them to love the outdoors. Once they grew a little older, he began taking them hunting. At first, just for small animals, like rabbits and squirrels, and then eventually for deer.

One evening, he was preparing to take our youngest daughter hunting the following morning. Early. Really early. Like 4:00 a.m. Because apparently 4:00 in the morning is the ideal time for hunters to trek into the woods. So, he was getting everything ready ahead of time because there would be no time to get things ready in the wee hours of the morning. He ran through his mental checklist. Guns and ammo: check. Camo backpack: check. Hand warmers, snacks, cover scent, and extra jacket: check. Coffee and hot chocolate: on the counter and ready to be made in the morning. Hunting licenses: Uh-oh! He had his hunting license, but could not find our daughter's. He knew it had to be somewhere! They had been hunting the previous week and he remembered having it at that time. He seemed to recall putting the license in a safe place. Too safe, apparently, because now he couldn't find it. And so, the hunt for the hunting license began!

First, we looked in all the obvious places: his wallet, jacket pockets, and that basket on the kitchen counter where everything seemed to end up. No luck. The hunt continued. We looked on the bookshelf and in the kitchen pantry. We rummaged between couch cushions and under the furniture. We searched in bedrooms, in bathrooms, and every room of the house. We looked in dresser drawers and on the laundry room floor. I rooted around on top of the refrigerator, because why not? But all I found up there was dust! I even sifted through the garbage. Yuck, by the way! I was beginning to feel like Indiana Jones on a treasure hunt. But without the whip. Or hat. And I didn't have a treasure map. But I sure could have used one. We searched the entire house, from top to bottom, but we came up empty-handed. Except for the dust. I got a handful of that!

By this point, we had just about given up hope of finding that elusive hunting license. So, at 9:30 p.m., my husband reluctantly decided the only thing he could do was drive to Wal-Mart and purchase another one. But for some reason, I wasn't ready to abandon the search just yet. I convinced my husband to give it one more try. As he headed to the basement to search, I decided to pray. Now why hadn't I thought of that an hour ago? We should have prayed before we rummaged through every corner of the house. After all, God cares about the smallest details, even a lost (or misplaced) hunting license. While my husband searched the basement, I walked through the house and asked God to help us find the license. I asked for his guidance and direction. I didn't look in any more cupboards or drawers. I just prayed. I made my way through the house, down the stairs, and to the basement.

And there stood my husband, triumphantly holding a small piece of paper in his right hand. He had found the hunting license! The search was over. I asked him where it had been hiding. His answer? In his Bible! Seriously, I am not making this up. He found it hidden in his waterproof camouflaged Bible, which was tucked inside his camo backpack. We had spent over an hour looking for something that wasn't lost! It was safe all along, hidden within the pages of God's Word.

There is an obvious lesson to be learned here. All that we want, all that we need, all we are searching for in this life can be found in God's Word. The Bible holds all the answers. But we often search somewhere else—anywhere else—for whatever it is we are looking for. We seek answers from social media. Or we Google it, because Google is always right, right? (Insert sarcasm here.) We read self-help books and listen to the ramblings of self-proclaimed experts. Or we seek advice from a friend—which isn't necessarily a bad thing, but it becomes wrong when we seek only a friend's opinion and neglect God's Word altogether. When we search for answers in worldly things, and not in God's Word, we will end up embarking on a perpetual treasure hunt. We will never find what we are looking for because what we are searching for can only be found in God, and in the pages of his Word.

In fact, Jeremiah 29:13 says, "You will seek me and find me when you seek me with all your heart." That is a guarantee straight from God's Word! God can be found. All you need to do is look for him. Jesus tells us to "ask and it will be given to you; seek and you will find; knock and the door will be opened to you. For everyone who asks receives; the one who seeks finds; and to the one who knocks the door will be opened" (Matthew 7:7–8). Plain and simple truth.

If we seek God, we will find him. We just need to look in the right place. His Word is our treasure map. No more searching through drawers or cupboards or social media or garbage cans. We will never be lost if we seek what we are looking for in the pages of God's Word.

Even if it is camouflaged!

PRAYER:

Lord, your Word is a guidebook for my life. Thank
you for providing all the answers I will ever
need. Help me to always seek you first!

FOUR

Sunday Morning Drama in the Church Parking Lot

I remember the early years of marriage. They were wonderful! Time spent being in love and gazing deeply into one another's eyes. Holding hands and kissing beneath the moonlight. Basking in the glow of our new and wondrous love. You know, the honeymoon phase! But it doesn't last forever, does it? Oh, don't get me wrong. I'm still madly in love with my husband. We are blessed to have a wonderful marriage. But those lovey-dovey, kissy-face, sappy-sweet moments don't last forever! Early in our relationship, my husband did all those chivalrous things. And he still does them, mostly. He let me enter a building in front of him. He carried the groceries into the house. He took out the trash. And he always opened the car door for me. Except one time . . . .

One Sunday morning, about a year into our marriage, we decided to have a fight on our way to church. Well, I guess we didn't consciously decide. But nonetheless, we had a fight. I do not remember what we fought about. I just remember being irritated. And angry. And saying some not nice things. And my loving husband saying some not nice things. And then I crossed my arms and refused to speak to him. Somehow, I thought this was the best thing to do. I thought he would see how very upset I was and realize that he was completely wrong, and I was obviously right. And he would apologize profusely. I wasn't too smart back then. I also didn't stay silent very long!

As we pulled into the church parking lot, I realized my plan hadn't worked at all. In fact, it had failed miserably. I sat in silence and watched as my husband parked the car, opened his door, got out of the car, shut his door, and walked directly across the parking lot and straight through the front doors of the church. Without me! What was this? How dare he leave me in the car! Alone. Still angry. With my arms crossed. How dare he walk into church without me! How rude! And embarrassing! What was I going to do? I looked quickly around the parking lot to see if any churchgoers had witnessed my great embarrassment. Thankfully, I didn't see anyone. Now I needed a plan. My very first thought was to hike up my skirt, quickly jump into the driver's seat, speed out of the parking lot, and head straight for home. And that's just what I would have done—if I had the car keys. Apparently, my husband shoved the keys into his pocket when he made his hasty exit from the vehicle. Not only did he leave me alone in the car, but he also left me stranded in the parking lot.

Now what would I do? I could crawl into the backseat and lay on the floor. But there was no way I would be comfortable crouching between the seats for an hour. Or two. I couldn't take the chance on the pastor being long-winded. I couldn't just sit there for everyone to see. I realized there really was no escape. I would actually have to go into the building! But there was no way was I going to march through the doors of that church without my husband by my side. There would be too many questions from those "well-meaning" church ladies. I would just have to slip in the back door.

I perused the parking lot once more to see if there were any stragglers. There was no one in sight. Perfect! I quickly stepped out of the car and flung the door shut behind me as I made my way swiftly around the back of the brick building. I rounded the corner and made a beeline for the door. I stopped only long enough to peek through the window. There was no one in the back hallway. I opened the door, stepped into the building, and all but ran into the lady's restroom, which thankfully was only a few steps from the entryway. Success! I had made it from the car to the bathroom completely unnoticed. No one would ever have to know of my embarrassing experience.

Now that I was safely inside the building, I needed another plan. I would wait a minute or two, flush the toilet just for show (in case any of those "well-meaning" church ladies were lingering nearby), wash my hands, exit the restroom, then head down the hall to find my husband. I would plaster a smile on my face and act like everything was normal. I would pretend that nothing out of the ordinary had happened. Like my husband hadn't left me alone and abandoned and angry in the parking lot with my arms crossed and steam coming out of my ears. I'd just act like everything was perfect and spiffy and fine and dandy!

That would work, right? It had to work! So that is just what I did. I strolled down the hall, through the foyer, and straight into the sanctuary, where I found my husband chatting with some friends, seemingly oblivious to the ordeal I had just been through. Figures. He was fine! Me, not so much. I was still irritated. But I pretended I was just as fine as he was. I faked a huge smile and slid into the pew next to my loving husband. After all, I certainly didn't want anyone to know my marriage was less than perfect.

Why, you ask? Why didn't I want anyone to know I had a fight with my husband on the way to church and he left me stranded in the parking lot? Well, I wouldn't have admitted it at the time, but now that I'm older and wiser (I hope), I can. Pride. The answer is pride. Scripture says, "When pride comes, then comes disgrace, but with humility comes wisdom" (Proverbs 11:2). Why is pride such a hard horse to wrangle? And just what is pride, anyway? In a biblical sense, pride simply means preferring your own will over God's will. To be prideful is to have an unreasonably high opinion of oneself. And that is just what I had. I didn't want anyone to think my marriage was less than perfect. Especially those "well-meaning" church ladies. I didn't want them talking about me behind their church bulletins.

I thought it was important to portray an appearance of perfection. Honestly, not for the sake of my marriage or my husband, but for myself. My own self-image. My own appearance. My own pride. Because, in my misguided opinion, a perfect marriage reflected well upon me. My character. My success as a wife. I did indeed have an inflated idea of my own importance. And I wanted to maintain that image. At any cost. But Proverbs 16:18 reminds us that "pride goes before destruction, a haughty spirit before a fall." Haughty is another one of those fun words. It simply means thinking higher of yourself than you should. I had placed myself on a high horse. But eventually I took a fall and learned how to wrangle my pride. Pride brings disgrace, but humility brings wisdom. In that order. Humility simply means to humble yourself. Yielding to God and putting his will above your own shows a humble heart. It takes practice. And patience. But humility yields a great reward: wisdom.

I'd like to say I'm always humble, but I'm not. I'd like to say I'm never prideful, but I am. Sometimes. I have gained much wisdom since the early years of my marriage. I've learned to keep my mouth shut. Sometimes. I have learned to put the needs of my husband above my own. I've learned to think less highly of myself. I've learned that God's ways are far greater than my own.

And I've learned it's a good idea to wear pants to church, just in case I have to do the fifty-yard dash across the parking lot!

PRAYER:

Dear Lord, you are so patient with me! I'm sorry
for the times I think too highly of myself. Help me
to exercise wisdom and display humility. Thank
you for loving me, even when I am foolish.

FIVE

Never Underestimate a Speedy Two-Year-Old

My husband lost our daughter at the Wal-Mart. Yes, you read that right. When my youngest daughter was nearly two years old, my husband took her and our four-year-old daughter shopping. They went in search of a new television. Ours had died earlier in the day and we wanted to get a new one right away because, let's be honest, sometimes letting the girls watch a thirty-minute animated show with talking animals or singing vegetables was the only break I got all day!

So, my darling husband set out in search of a new TV. And, bonus for me, he took the girls with him so I could have a little uninterrupted peace and quiet. I don't remember exactly how I spent my free time. It was a long time ago. Most likely I ate chocolate peanut butter ice-cream and read a book. Anyway, I enjoyed my alone time. For as long as it lasted. And then they returned home and my peaceful moment was over.

My chatty four-year-old jumped out of the car, ran up to me, and said, "Mama, Daddy lost sissy at the Wal-Mart." Umm . . . say what now? Surely, I had not heard her correctly. So, I asked her to repeat what she had said. And the same words came out of her mouth the second time around. "Daddy lost sissy at the Wal-Mart." My blood began to boil. Smoke was coming out of my ears. My "Mama Bear" came roaring out from within. I ran to the window, threw back the curtain, and peered outside, desperately trying to catch a glimpse of my baby. I saw Daddy getting my sweet girl out of her car seat. Oh, praise the Lord! My baby wasn't lost! I could see her with my own eyes. My blood pressure slowly began to drop, but I was still ready to roar. Daddy had a lot of explaining to do, the very moment he walked into the house. Because I had questions. Lots and lots of questions. And Daddy better have some exceptionally good answers. Because Daddy was in big trouble.

I didn't take my eyes off my baby until my husband stepped through the doorway. I immediately pulled her out of his arms and smothered her in kisses. I squeezed her until she squirmed, then reluctantly put her down. She ran off to play with her sister, without a care in the world. I turned my full attention to my husband, fully prepared to unleash my inner "Mama Bear." His wide eyes told me he knew that our four-year-old had told on him, and he knew I was about to blow my top! But before I could even open my mouth, he quickly began to explain.

He was at Wal-Mart. He had put our youngest daughter in the seat of the shopping cart. Our older girl walked alongside the cart, holding her daddy's hand. They went to the electronics department and he found the TV he wanted, but it wouldn't fit in the cart with our daughter sitting in the seat. So, Daddy decided it would be a good idea to take our two-year-old baby girl out of the seat and place her on the floor. In a crowd. In the middle of the Wal-Mart. His intention was to quickly fold in the seat, place the TV in the cart, and then pick her up and carry her. But he underestimated our girl. She was smart. And fast. And apparently adventurous!

After placing the TV in the cart, he looked down and our baby girl was gone! Nowhere to be seen. Our older girl suddenly pointed and said, "There goes sissy!" as she rounded the corner into the ladies' clothing department. Daddy quickly pursued with our four-year-old in tow. As they rounded the corner, they were just in time to see the little one disappear around another corner. For the next ten minutes, Daddy was in hot pursuit of a slippery two-year-old. Or was she the roadrunner? She kept giving him the slip. Along the way, Daddy asked no less than seven employees if they had seen our daughter. One employee offered to help with the search, while another alerted management to begin a lockdown of the store! A lockdown! Because my baby girl was missing! I nearly died. Seriously, I think I saw Saint Peter.

Anyway, after frantically searching for a misplaced two-year-old while trying to keep track of a four-year-old, Daddy finally caught a break. A friendly female employee suddenly came walking toward my husband, carrying our little sprinter—who, by the way, had a huge smile on her face. God bless that woman! After making sure our daughter did, in fact, belong to my husband, she handed her over and the lockdown was lifted. After paying for the TV, Daddy headed home, with both of his daughters in tow. Thank the Lord.

After my husband explained everything, he smiled at me and said, "But she's fine." And, as every mother since the dawn of time knows, this did nothing to make me feel better. Don't get me wrong. I was beyond grateful that my baby girl was safe and unharmed and no longer lost in the Wal-Mart. But I was still beyond angry that this happened in the first place. And it took a very, very, very long time for my anger and irritation to dissipate. But my anger did go away. And I forgave my husband, eventually. After all, I knew he didn't purposely lose our child at the Wal-Mart. But Mama Bear needed some time to process!

I wondered what went through the mind of my little mischievous girl. She obviously had no idea of the potential danger she faced. She had no fear of the unknown. Running away from her father didn't frighten her one bit. My sweet little daughter obviously didn't realize that running away from her father was dangerous. She wasn't mature enough to see the potential perils. Staying close to her daddy's side offered her protection, because she is much safer in his presence. Thankfully, no harm came to her during her brief stint as Dora the Explorer.

In much the same way, running away from God is dangerous. Just ask Jonah. He is perhaps the most famous runner in the Bible. Simply put, Jonah ran from God because he did not want to do what God was asking of him. He thought he could hide from the Lord. He was wrong. He didn't know that running from God would land him inside the gut of a big fish! But inside that stinky stomach is where Jonah finally got right with the Lord.

In Jonah chapter one, God tells Jonah to go to Nineveh and preach against wickedness. But did Jonah listen? Nope! In verse three it says, "But Jonah ran away from the LORD and headed for Tarshish." He went down to Joppa, found a ship, paid the fare, went aboard, and headed for Tarshish to flee from the Lord. Wow! He was serious about running away from God! But God was having none of it. Chapter one goes on to say that the Lord sent a great wind on the sea, a violent storm arose, the sailors tossed Jonah into the water, the storm ceased, and Jonah was swallowed by a big fish. Eww! In chapter two we learn that from inside the belly of the fish, Jonah began praying and pouring his heart out to God. And probably questioning his recent life choices! And after three days and three nights, the Lord released Jonah from his digestive prison: "And the LORD commanded the fish, and it vomited Jonah onto dry land" (2:10). Eww again!

But Jonah's time inside the stomach of the fish was time well spent.

Because this time, when the Lord told Jonah to go to Nineveh, he went! We can learn an important lesson from Jonah. Running from God is useless, because you can't outrun God! Running from God is simply not necessary, because God always knows what is best for us.

So why do we run? Sometimes it's a fear of the unknown. Or, perhaps, a fear of what is already known! Other times we run because we do not trust that God knows what is best. Or we think our plan is better than God's plan for our lives. Or, like my two-year-old daughter, we are simply not mature enough to have a healthy fear of God.

Time to stop running. It is futile. And you just might end up in the belly of a fish.

Or even worse, lost and alone at the Wal-Mart!

PRAYER:

Lord, you are truly a loving Father. I know you are always with me, even when I lose my way, or when I wander off on my own. Thank you for your faithfulness and loving guidance.

SIX

The Peace and Patience of a Blind Beagle

My dog is blind. She gets around well for not being able to see. She also has diabetes, which is actually what caused the blindness. Having diabetes means she drinks a lot of water. Which means she has to pee a lot. Which means she has to go outside a lot. More than the average dog. And honestly, taking her out so many times a day can be very inconvenient. I know that sounds mean, but it's true! I can't just open the door and let her run. She's blind. She will get lost! This has happened more than once.

Taking my dog out ten times a day means putting my shoes on ten times a day. And my coat, if it's cold. And walking her down the long deck steps. And making sure she doesn't fall off the bridge. And guiding her away from the prickly holly tree. And making sure she doesn't step in her own poop. This has happened more than once.

When it's raining, taking her out is an even bigger hassle. Balancing an umbrella in one hand and holding a leash in the other hand with a dog pulling to get down the long, wet, slippery steps does not make for an easy time. I have fallen down those steps. This has happened more than once.

So, my genius husband came up with the perfect solution! He

attached a retractable leash to the front porch rail. When the dog needs to go out, we just open the door, clip the leash onto her collar, and let her go! All by herself! Down the front steps. No need to accompany her outside! This is perfect for when it's raining. Or really cold. Or it's late at night. Or very early in the morning. Or for any time, really! We still take her out and walk her a few times a day, but this new setup makes it so much easier for everyone—including the pooch!

Having the ability to let her go outside, on her own, and not get lost has been wonderful. At first, she was hesitant to walk down the steps. Probably because she couldn't see them. But now she just heads right down the steps until she feels the grass under her paws. She seems to enjoy the little bit of freedom she has to be outside on her own. She feels no sense of urgency. She pees when she's ready, poops if she needs to, then walks back up the stairs on her own sweet time. Sometimes we find her lying on the porch, basking in the sun, with the wind blowing on her face, ears flapping in the breeze.

The one drawback to this otherwise perfect system is that we have to shovel poop away from the porch or someone will step in it. This has happened more than once. And when I say we have to shovel the poop, I mean my husband has to shovel the poop. He's in charge of poop removal. He scoops the poop with a snow shovel that he keeps propped against the side of the porch.

One morning, my husband clipped the dog onto the leash just as my daughters were leaving for school. We both had a little time before we had to leave the house, so we sat down to enjoy a cup (or two) of coffee. Just as we were getting ready to leave, we realized we had never let the pup back inside. Sometimes she'll scratch at the door if we leave her out there too long. But we hadn't heard any scratching. Oh well. She was probably just taking a nap on the porch.

But as I opened the door to let her in, I could see she was definitely not taking a nap! She was perched on the second step from the bottom, still attached to her leash, which was attached to the snow shovel! Somehow, our sweet little blind beagle had managed to get the retractable leash wrapped around the handle of the shovel—not once, but twice! The bottom of the shovel was wedged in the ground by the steps and the handle was leaning against the porch rail. About seven inches of leash separated the pup from the shovel. Don't be alarmed. She was not being strangled; she was fine. She was just stuck. But she didn't seem to mind one bit! That's right. Our poor little blind dog was trapped on the porch steps, stuck to a snow shovel, frozen in place, unable to move. And she was fine! She didn't howl, or cry, or whimper. She just sat there. Peacefully. Like the Queen of England surveying her royal kingdom. Like it was a normal thing to be wearing a snow shovel. Like she didn't have a care in the world. She just sat there calmly. Waiting to be rescued.

I have to admit, I laughed. It was hilarious! I called my husband over to look, and he laughed, too. I have no idea how one little blind beagle managed to get so tangled up without strangling herself. She must be super talented. Or maybe just plain lucky! Maybe she wasn't concerned because she wasn't aware of her circumstances. After all, she is blind and obviously couldn't see that she was stuck to a snow shovel. If she actually knew what was happening, she probably would have flipped out! But she did not flip out. She just sat there calmly, unaware of the danger, peacefully waiting to be rescued.

How many times am I in a precarious situation, fully aware of my surroundings, knowing that trouble is in sight? How do I react when I unexpectedly find myself attached to something I do not want to be tied to? Do I patiently wait for the Lord to rescue me? Do I close my eyes in trust, turning away from the danger, and choosing instead to focus on God?

I hate to admit it, but if I found myself bound to a snow shovel, stuck in place, and unable to move, I don't think I'd sit patiently and wait to be rescued. In fact, I'd probably panic. And yell for help. Rather loudly. Until my husband came to my rescue.

In the book of Psalms, God asks us to wait on him. "Wait for the LORD; be strong and take heart and wait for the LORD" (Psalm 27:14). And "I wait for the LORD, my whole being waits, and in his word I put my hope" (Psalm 130:5).

Waiting on God's timing can be difficult. I, for one, am not so good at waiting. I tend to be a little impatient (or a lot impatient, depending on the situation)! I want to be rescued immediately. I do not want to suffer. But patiently waiting yields its reward. Just think of my poor little dog. If she had not been patient in waiting to be rescued, she could have gotten hurt. If she had tried to free herself, she may have gotten knocked in the head with a snow shovel. Or worse!

God always sees the big picture. He always knows what's best for me. Sometimes, when he asks me to wait, it's not because he wants me to be stuck in a precarious place for the rest of my life. It's simply because he knows what is best for me. He can see the danger I'm wrapped up in. And he alone knows the best way to untangle it!

So, the next time I find myself tied up in knots, I'll take a cue from my dog. I will close my eyes, choose to trust, and patiently wait for the Lord to rescue me.

But just to be safe, I'm going to move that snow shovel!

PRAYER:

Dear Lord, I'm so glad you always see the big picture.
Thank you for caring enough to orchestrate every detail
of my life. Help me to close my eyes and trust you.

SEVEN

Cream Cheese is Better than Butter on a Bagel

It all started with a container of spreadable cream cheese.

One morning, I was making breakfast for my daughter. I popped a bagel into the toaster and grabbed a tub of cream cheese from the fridge. I opened the lid and peered inside, into the depths of a nearly empty container. It was like a canyon in there. I think I heard an echo!

I was instantly irritated. You see, this is one of my pet peeves. Not cream cheese, specifically, but using all or almost all of something and not writing it on the grocery list. It drives me nuts! Because then what happens is this exact thing. No more cream cheese! Or barely enough for half a bagel, which is what I scraped out of the tub.

My husband and daughters were standing in the kitchen. I looked to them for an explanation. No one volunteered to explain. Fueled by my irritation, I asked who had used all the cream cheese and did not write it on the grocery list. No response. Silence. I think I heard crickets. This is also one of my pet peeves. Not answering when I ask a question.

Clearly, I wasn't getting through to them. So, I thought an object lesson would be a good idea. I picked up the tub, walked three paces across the kitchen, and showed them the inside of the container. I thought surely this would do the trick. They would see that I was not exaggerating. They would see the emptiness. But, no! My husband's response: "It's not empty. There's still some in there."

Yes. Yes, there was. There was enough cream cheese to cover the tip of my pinky finger. There was enough to spread on a grape. And technically, there was enough left in the container to say it wasn't completely empty!

But technically, that was not the point.

So, I proceeded to explain why we should write things on the grocery list before they run out. That if you see something is low, it is common courtesy to write it on the list so that I know we are almost out and I can buy more and we are not left with an empty container of cream cheese and no one has to choke down a dry bagel!

Is this too much to ask? I think not!

As my daughters left for school, my husband stayed behind. And for the next twenty minutes, we politely discussed my irritation over the cream cheese situation. And when I say politely, I mean not so much (at least for me . . . I was still worked up).

Really, it's just common courtesy. If you use up all or almost all of the cream cheese or peanut butter or toilet paper for goodness' sake, just write it on the grocery list! It is not hard to do! I always have a magnetic list pad stuck to the side of the refrigerator. It has been in the same place for the last fourteen years. Everyone knows it's there. Everyone in my house can read and write. There is really no excuse for not doing this!

Except sometimes there is.

I calmed down long enough to listen to what my husband had to say about the cream cheese. He said, "We are not perfect. Sometimes we forget. No one purposely left an almost empty container in the fridge. Someone probably meant to write cream cheese on the grocery list, but got distracted." He's so wise. Annoying, right?

And even though our daughters are my flesh and blood, they don't always see things the same way I do. And my husband—well, we see lots of things differently. An empty cream cheese container does not bother him one bit! And that is okay. Not everyone will see things the same way as me. I am a very organized, detail-oriented person. I like things done a certain way. I like things to be in order. I may be a little controlling.

My husband and children are good, loving people with good hearts and good intentions. I'm sure they do not intentionally do things to irritate me. (At least I hope they don't!) Maybe instead of being so quick to become irritated, I can try being patient with my people. Great idea, right? And maybe I can learn to overlook the small things, knowing the people I love are mostly good and kind and responsible. After all, the Bible says in Ephesians 4:2, "Be completely humble and gentle; be patient, bearing with one another in love."

This includes being patient with my children when they forget to put their socks in the hamper, or they use up all the shampoo (and don't write it on the list). Being patient with my husband when he forgets to take his boots off and tracks mud and dirt and dried leaves across the living room floor.

Why? Because I would want them to be patient with me.

Matthew 7:12 says, "So in everything, do to others what you would have them do to you." I would not want my people to yell at me over something as insignificant as cream cheese. As delicious as it is, it is not worth hurting someone over. My hope is that they would bear with me as I'm learning to bear with them. To love one another, to graciously forgive, and to be merciful when mistakes are made.

A magnetic list pad still hangs on my refrigerator. And people do, in fact, write items on that list. Sometimes. Other times, I try to lovingly remind them to put it on the list.

Because running out of cream cheese is clearly not an option!

PRAYER:

Lord, you are loving and merciful. Thank you for being
patient with me when I am so undeserving. Help me
to extend that same love and mercy to others.

EIGHT

Hot Pink Denim Shines Brighter in the Glow of a Blue Light

Did you ever shop at K-Mart back in the day? I shopped there all the time when I was a kid. I remember taking many trips to the K-Mart on Saturday mornings. It was great! You could buy practically anything there: blue jeans, toilet paper, cereal, snow tires . . . There was even a little snack bar where you could order a delicious hot dog or a warm, buttery soft pretzel. And don't forget the Slush Puppie, which was a shaved-ice frozen drink that came in many different fruity flavors. My favorite was blue. I don't remember what the actual flavor was. Probably blue raspberry. But I loved it. In fact, I loved it so much that I would drink it way too fast and get brain freeze. Then my tongue would be blue for hours afterward. Bright blue. Like I had chewed on a magic marker. But I didn't care! Actually, having a blue tongue was one of the things I liked most about the Slush Puppie!

But my favorite thing about K-Mart was the "Blue Light Special." This was a sales promotion that announced the sale of a specific item by flashing a blue light. An employee wheeled out a cart with a flashing blue light and placed the cart beside the sale item. Then a voice came over the loudspeaker and said, "Attention K-Mart shoppers. Sale on tube socks in aisle four. Two packs for the price of one." And then almost everyone flocked to aisle four, whether they needed tube socks or not. You never knew what was going to be on sale. It was so exciting! That flashing blue light had the power to make you believe you needed whatever was on sale! I mean, really. Who needs twenty cans of SpaghettiOs? Buy nineteen cans and get one free! But sometimes there were great deals. All swimwear, fifty percent off. Or, buy one box of Lucky Charms and get a second one free. Who doesn't love Lucky Charms? They're magically delicious!

When I was twelve years old, there was one particular item I wanted to buy. It was a hot pink denim jacket. Don't judge, it was the eighties. I loved that jacket! Every Saturday for a month, I would try it on and ask my mom if I could buy it. I even had some birthday money saved up that I was willing to contribute. I don't remember how much it cost, but it must have been more than my mom wanted to spend.

One Saturday, I entered the store and headed straight for the junior's department, in search of my beloved pink jean jacket. It was there in the usual spot, but it was the only one hanging on the rack! Oh no! The only one left! I quickly snatched it off the rack and checked the size. Hallelujah! It was my size! It was meant to be! Now I just had to convince my mom to finally buy the bright pink beauty. I needed to come up with a plan. And fast! I could just ask my mom, but I had tried that before. More than once. And she had said no. More than once. But I really, really, really wanted that jacket! I needed a plan. As I walked around the store, tightly clutching that precious hot pink denim, I suddenly had an inspiration. The Blue Light Special! It was my only hope! Maybe today's sale would be on pink jean jackets. Maybe they would be fifty percent off. Or seventy-five percent. Heck, why not ninety percent? Or maybe, just maybe, today would be the luckiest day of my life and the voice on the loudspeaker would say, "Attention K-Mart shoppers. For one minute only, all pink jean jackets are free!" Okay, so this had never happened before, but a girl could dream, couldn't she?

I decided to follow an employee around the store for a while to see if she suddenly pulled out the magical cart. I kept a safe distance between myself and the clerk. While she stocked bottles in the shampoo aisle, I looked at hairspray in the next row. As she straightened cans in the grocery aisle, I suddenly became interested in the price of baked beans. I followed her around the store like I was a covert spy on a secret mission, all the while clinging to the hot pink denim. I'm fairly certain the clerk never spotted me. But what did I know? I was a twelve-year-old girl stalking an employee through the K-Mart! The clerk probably thought I was nuts.

I roamed the store in eager expectation for what seemed like four hours. But in reality, it was probably only twenty minutes. But that blue light never flashed! The intercom remained silent, except for the elevator music. And sadly, I realized I would never own my hot pink beauty. I slowly turned my feet in the direction of the junior's department and began the long walk across the store to return my beloved treasure. My dream faded as I placed my pretty pink jean jacket back on the rack. I may or may not have shed a tear. My sadness was short-lived, however. Just then, my sister ran up and said, "Hey, Mom said we can get a Slush Puppie!" Well, I wouldn't be wearing pink denim, but my tongue sure would be blue! At least for the next two hours!

The "Blue Light Special" brings to mind the triumphant return of Jesus. We do not know when it will happen. But we do know for certain that it will happen! In reference to his return, Jesus says, "But about that day or hour no one knows, not even the angels in heaven, nor the Son, but only the Father. Be on guard! Be alert! You do not know when that time will come" (Mark 13:32–33). We have the assurance that Jesus will return. That is a promise! But we are not given a date or time. That is why we must stand guard. Be alert, and wait in eager expectation.

Sometimes we lose sight of this. We go about our lives, searching for something to occupy our time while we wait. We fill our lives with work, relationships, distractions, and things. We wander the aisles, in search of something—anything—to put our hope in. SpaghettiOs, tube socks, or a hot pink jean jacket. But these are merely distractions from the ultimate prize. And no, it's not the denim jacket. It is, of course, our Lord and Savior Jesus Christ! The twelve-year-old me put her hope in the wrong thing. I clung tightly to that bright pink dream while searching for that elusive blue light. My hope was misplaced. The grown-up, forty-something me knows that Jesus is the only true hope. And if I cling as tightly to him as I once did to that jean jacket, I will one day be rewarded with the ultimate "Blue Light Special."

I never did get my hot pink beauty. But that's okay. Because one day I will walk streets of gold!

And suddenly I have a craving for blue raspberry!

PRAYER:

Lord, you are so generous. You are the giver of
all good things. My treasure is found in you.
Thank you for the promise of heaven.

NINE

Be Careful Where You Dump Your Undies

Did you ever do something in anger? Something you regretted? Maybe not instantly, but eventually regretted, at some point in the future. Maybe only five minutes in the future. Or two hours, or two days. But nonetheless, you ended up regretting it. And then you wished you could go back in time and get a do-over. To set things right. Like Marty McFly going back (or was it forward?) to Hill Valley to save Doc Brown. Where's a DeLorean when you need one?

I once got so angry at my husband that I took the entire contents of his underwear drawer and dumped it outside. On the front lawn. For all the world to see. I dumped his undies in a heap. Right at the end of the driveway. Every blessed pair!

I can't even remember why I was so mad at him. I'm sure we must have argued about something. And I'm certain he must have said something insensitive. And I'm confident that he was totally wrong. And I was absolutely right. Which is why I felt fully justified in dumping his drawers by the driveway.

I thought, *This will show him I mean business! He can't talk to me like that! He hurt my feelings so I will just march down the hall to our bedroom, remove the top right dresser drawer, proceed directly out the front door, and plop his underwear on the lawn!* Because that will make him angry! That will get him good!

What was I thinking?

It did not go according to plan. I somehow imagined my husband running quickly outside to scoop up his shorts, cheeks red with embarrassment, shame radiating from his face. He would see his Fruit of the Looms laying in the great outdoors and would understand how much he hurt me. It would be his lightbulb moment! He would suddenly proclaim, "Ah! Now I understand!"

But that never happened. There was no walk of shame to reclaim the undies. No red cheeks of embarrassment. No apologies.

Oh no, my friend. His reaction was completely opposite of what I had hoped! I'm talking night and day opposite. This man did not care that his underpants were piled outside in a heap on the grass. He said, "I don't care. I'll wear the same pair all week. And then I'll turn them inside out."

And in that moment, I believed him. I knew it was not an empty threat. I knew that he would, in fact, wear the same pair every blessed day. For seven days straight! And then he would turn them inside out.

And that was when I regretted my actions. Just moments before I had been so proud of myself. Proud! I thought my plan was so clever! But clearly, I had not thought it through. I had acted in anger. In haste. Why did I dump this man's underwear in our front yard for all the world to see? Well, at least all of the neighbors! I wished I had never touched the underwear at all. What was I going to do?

I did the only thing I could. I took the walk of shame to undo what I had done. I went outside and began picking up the undies as fast as I could, keeping my head down, and praying the neighbors wouldn't see me. I gathered them all up. Every last pair. And then I marched into the house and promptly deposited them in the washing machine.

I cannot say for certain, but as I marched down the hall on my way to the laundry room, I think I saw my husband grinning from ear to ear. I may have heard laughter, too. And he may or may not have been doing a happy dance!

Again, clearly, I had not thought this through. Not only did I have to pick the underwear up myself, but I had to wash them, too! I had created more work for myself. Good grief!

And there it was! Full blown regret. And shame. And a little anger at my own stupidity, and the fact that I now had more laundry to do!

Scripture says, "My dear brothers and sisters, take note of this: Everyone should be quick to listen, slow to speak and slow to become angry" (James 1:19).

Looks like I still have a little work to do in this area. I have to admit, this is tough for me! As tough as shoe leather. Being slow to speak does not come naturally to me. I am a fast talker. Not like a speed talker, or that guy from the Matchbox car commercials. Remember him? No, I'm more like a quick responder. And when I'm talking, I'm usually not listening. Although I am capable of doing both at the same time. But for the most part, when my mouth is working, my ears are not!

And that anger! It is so hard to control. Sometimes I feel fully justified in my anger. I feel a righteous indignation. Okay, self-righteous! Proverbs reminds us that "fools give full vent to their rage, but the wise bring calm in the end" (29:11). Yep, that's me! I'm a fool.

How can this be? But there it is, right there in God's Word. It's the truth. I need to heed God's instruction, put a muzzle on my mouth, and get that anger under control! I do not want to be a fool. I want to be wise. And controlled. And I never want to pick up underwear off the lawn in broad daylight again!

PRAYER:

Lord, I lose my temper far too often. Thank you for loving me, even when I act like a fool. Help me to keep myself under control. I want to honor you with my words and actions.

TEN

The Great Chicken Escape

We have chickens. A backyard flock of hens. They're good little egg layers, as long as they have feed, water, and plenty of sunlight. We keep them at the back of our property in an eight-by-fifteen-foot enclosed pen. So, I guess they are not technically free range. But that's just because I do not want chicken poop in my yard. Eww! But the pen is large enough for them to roam around and scratch in the dirt. There is also a henhouse that serves as a place to roost at night and find shelter during rainy weather.

Our chickens live a simple life and seem to be happy birds. Most days. But sometimes they have a bad day. Like the day they were attacked by a Cooper's Hawk. That brazen bird flew right into the opening on the side of the henhouse and killed two of our hens. I'll spare you the details. It was not a pretty sight. One of the hens managed to get out of the pen and ran screaming into the woods with flapping wings and feathers flying. We searched for her but she was nowhere to be found. We thought she was lost for good. But hours later, we found her at the edge of the yard, hiding under a giant azalea bush. She had crazy eyes. We tried to coax her out but she would not budge. She stayed in there for seven hours and did not come out until dark! My husband hawk-proofed the pen and we haven't had a problem since.

Sometimes we let the chickens out of the pen to roam around the yard because they will eat ticks and other insects, which is great for us. Nobody likes ticks. But we only let them out occasionally. Because of the poop. Eww! But we have to supervise them because our hens are not too bright and they get lost easily. Every now and then, one of those birds will escape the pen on her own. This happened once when my husband went into the pen to fill the feeder. He must have left the gate open a little bit because we suddenly saw one of those crazy hens running across the yard. She looked very pleased with herself. She puffed up her chest and pecked at the grass and then she threw a sassy glance over her wing. I'm pretty sure she was smiling. Oh, how soon she forgot the dangers she could encounter outside the safety of her pen.

We live in the woods and there are always predatory animals nearby: foxes, coyotes (sometimes we hear them howling at night), and let's not forget those hawks! Okay, so technically the chickens were attacked while inside their pen, but we hawk-proofed it, so now being inside the pen is definitely safer than being outside the pen. It was beginning to get dark and we knew we needed to get that chicken back into the pen for her own safety. My daughter is a very good chicken catcher, so I asked for her help. She did her thing and tried to catch it. But chickens are faster than they look and she had trouble cornering the bird. So, I offered to help.

We quickly formulated a plan. I hid behind a tree while my daughter circled wide to come up from behind the bird. It would be a sneak attack! The plan was to chase the chicken in my direction, and when she got close, I would jump out from behind the tree, thereby scaring the bird and forcing her to turn and run the other direction, right back toward my daughter. Yep, that was the plan.

But that is not what happened. Oh, we scared the chicken, alright. She squawked and flailed and ran willy-nilly in the wrong direction! We chased after her, squealing and flailing our arms in hot pursuit. But alas, the bird was too fast and she gave us the slip. As she ran full speed ahead into the wide-open yard, she glanced at us over her wing with a look of triumph in her beady little eyes. I think I heard her singing, "Nanny, nanny, boo boo! You can't catch me!" Well, fine then. That slippery chicken could just stay outside the pen. We gave up and went inside. She would just have to fend for herself.

I know animals are supposed to have natural instincts, but I don't think our chickens have a lick of sense. That stupid hen didn't seem to know any better. But we should know better! God's love and protection are like that chicken wire fence. If we stay inside the security of the pen, we will be kept safe. If we stay within the protection of God's arms, we will be offered his security. But how do we do this? By reading God's Word and obeying his commands. By seeking to follow his will for our lives. By surrendering our will and choosing daily to trust him and live a life that is pleasing to him. If we love the Lord, we will obey his commands and choose to be obedient to him. By being obedient, we willingly place ourselves under his authority, under the shelter of his wings.

Psalm 91:1 says, "Whoever dwells in the shelter of the Most High will rest in the shadow of the Almighty." Verse four goes on to say, "He will cover you with his feathers, and under his wings you will find refuge; his faithfulness will be your shield and rampart." Actually, you should take a minute to read all of Psalm 91. It is really good stuff! If you dwell in the Lord and remain in his presence, he will shelter you under his wings. This does not mean that you will never face danger. But just like that wayward chicken, you have a better chance of receiving God's protection if you choose to dwell in him, if you "stay inside the pen." If you step outside of the fence, you willingly remove yourself from the shelter of God's arms, leaving you vulnerable to attacks from predatory creatures. Maybe not a coyote or a Cooper's Hawk, but Satan. And he is far more dangerous!

Inside the pen is safer than outside the pen. Just ask my crazy chickens!

PRAYER:

Lord, you are the Almighty, El Shaddai. Thank you for offering me your divine protection. I want to stay in the shelter of your wings.

ELEVEN

A Squeaky Cot Makes for a Sleepless Night

When our oldest daughter was seventeen, near the end of her junior year of high school, we decided it was time to start looking at colleges, so we planned her first visit. The college she chose was only a six-hour drive from home. We thought it would be a fun trip for the whole family, so we took our younger daughter along as well. The visit was scheduled for Monday morning, so we headed out on Sunday afternoon. Our plan was to drive straight there on Sunday, stay the night at a hotel, then drive home Monday after the visit. Easy peasy.

We reserved one hotel room with two queen beds and a pull-out couch. But when we arrived, that is not what we found. There were two queen beds, but there was no pull-out couch. In fact, there was no couch at all. Oops! I thought for sure I had reserved a room with a pull-out couch. I had already told the girls they wouldn't have to share a bed. At seventeen and fifteen years old, they did not love the idea of being squished together in the same bed. No problem. Easy fix. We called down to the front desk and asked them to send up a rollaway bed. This idea seemed to appeal to the teenagers. That is, until the cot arrived and the hotel clerk wheeled it into the room. It was clunky. And squeaky. And old. Like from 1912. Or from whatever year rollaway beds were invented. Which by the looks of it was 1912. And the mattress was, shall we say, less than comfortable. It had old-time springs in it. Like from 1912. Seriously. Old springs. And very little padding. But my youngest daughter assured me that it would be fine and she was just glad to have a bed of her own. Great! Crisis averted!

When it was time for bed, we all climbed into our assigned locations. My husband and I were in one of the queen beds, our youngest daughter was on the cot that may have been on the Titanic, and college girl somehow managed to get the other queen bed to herself. This wouldn't be so bad. We'd all get a good night's sleep, enjoy the breakfast buffet in the morning, drive to the college, and have a lovely visit. Our daughter would be well on her way to making an informed decision about her future. Yep, that was the plan. Everything was working out fine. For about three minutes. And then I heard it. Squeak! Squeak! Squeak! Followed by a gigantic sigh! Not a small, dainty sigh. Nope, a ginormous exhaling-of-breath kind of sigh! Uh-oh. It seemed our girl on the cot was not enjoying her experience. I asked if she was alright and she assured me she was fine. Wonderful! Back to trying to fall asleep. This time everything was fine for about seven minutes, then more squeaking and sighing and loud breathing, followed by me asking if everything was alright. This pattern continued 345 times over the next fifty-two minutes. Or maybe it was only fifteen minutes. I can't say for sure.

At this point, it was quite obvious that our girl on the cot was certainly not going to get any sleep if she remained on the mattress from the Titanic. And I wasn't going to be getting any sleep because I'm a mom. And moms just don't sleep when their children are sighing loudly from across the room. And college girl wasn't sleeping because of all the noise. The only person who was sleeping was Dad!

Well, that was it. I had to do something. So, I told the little one to get in bed with the big one and just deal with it. At this point, there was more sighing and loud breathing. Mostly coming from me. I was tired and irritated, but I took the time to roll up a comforter to place down the middle of the bed to act as a barrier so the girls wouldn't have to touch each other. I thought this was a brilliant idea! But college girl did not. She flung herself, none too gently, and quite dramatically, to the far side of her edge of the bed. And then she sighed. Loudly. I ever-so-politely (insert sarcasm here) told her that she was welcome to sleep on the antique rollaway cot if she was less than satisfied with the new sleeping arrangement. She very quickly declined. Smart girl.

So now I had two girls in one queen bed, wide awake, clinging to their respective sides of the bed like life rafts. Well, fine. They could hang off the sides all night if they wanted. As long as they were quiet. I tried to go back to sleep. Truly, I did. But then the snoring began. Snoring! Coming from the only person in the room who was actually sleeping! You guessed it—Dad. Now, I am used to his snoring. But the girls, not so much. So, when a voice from the life raft called out "Daddy's snoring," I just said, "Welcome to my world." The voice continued, "But I can't sleep!" I replied, "Just stick your fingers in your ears and go to sleep!" I don't know how much time passed after that. I only know there was a mixture of snoring, sighing, and some kind of incessant humming coming from the mini fridge. I was not sleeping. The girls were not sleeping. No one was sleeping, except for Dad!

Sometime in the wee hours of the morning, around the 133rd sigh, I snapped! I flung back the covers, jumped out of bed, and shouted, "This is ridiculous! We have got to get some sleep! Someone is going to have to sleep on that cot, or on the floor, or in the bathtub! I really don't care! But we all need to get some sleep! Right now!" I was met with silence. No reply. Until Dad finally woke up. I guess my middle-of-the-night tirade was loud enough to rouse him from his slumber. He sat halfway up in bed and sleepily asked, "What's going on?" This would have been cute if it wasn't 1:30 in the morning. But it was. So, it wasn't cute. Just irritating.

But he had just woken up and had no idea what was happening. So, for his benefit, I recounted the past two hours while he was sleeping: the sighing and breathing and snoring and humming. He didn't say a word. He just got out of the comfy queen bed, walked to the other side of the room, and laid down on the cot. The antique, uncomfortable, squeaking cot from 1912. This man was my hero. He had saved the day. Well, the night. He is over six feet tall and the cot was probably only five-and-a-half feet long. His feet hung off the end. The cot squeaked as he shifted into place. There was no way he would sleep well. He would be sore in the morning. I felt bad for him. I started to tell him that I would sleep on the cot, but my words were cut short by the sound of snoring! He was already asleep, bless his heart! Now it was time for the rest of us to get some sleep. Our youngest daughter climbed into bed with me and our oldest somehow once again ended up with an entire bed to herself. It was dark so I couldn't be certain, but I'm fairly sure she fell asleep with a triumphant smile on her lips.

The next morning, we were all a little tired, but not nearly as tired as I was expecting, considering the chaos from the night before. We enjoyed cinnamon rolls at the breakfast buffet before heading off to the college. The campus was beautiful and the people were friendly. We took a tour, ate a nice lunch, and had meetings with three professors. College girl even got to play piano for one of them! It was a good experience, despite the fact that we were all starting to feel the effects of not enough sleep. As we got in the car to head home, we asked our daughter if she thought she could see herself attending this college. Her response: "Ehh . . . not really." Well, fine! That was just fine with me. I was too tired to care anyway. I just wanted to go home. And so, we drove home, six straight hours, and slept in our own beds!

This trip did not go exactly as I had planned. But isn't that how life is? So many times, I make plans and I expect those plans to go exactly as I have outlined them. I am a planner by nature. I like things to be nice and orderly and well thought out. But sometimes I forget to include God in those plans. Oh, it's not that I think I know more than God. Believe me, I don't! But sometimes I get a little ahead of myself. I don't always pray and ask God to guide my plans first. Sometimes I make a plan and then ask God to carry out the plans I've made. Wow! This is not how it should be. God's plans are far better than my plans. In his Word we read, "'For my thoughts are not your thoughts, neither are your ways my ways,' declares the LORD. 'As the heavens are higher than the earth, so are my ways higher than your ways and my thoughts than your thoughts'" (Isaiah 55:8–9). God's thoughts, God's plans, God's ways are far better than mine. He knows all things and sees all things. My limited brain cannot begin to comprehend the ways of God. My plans could never compare with the plans of God. I should pray and seek God's guidance before I start making plans.

James 4:13–15 says, "Now listen, you who say, 'Today or tomorrow we will go to this or that city, spend a year there, carry on business and make money.' Why, you do not even know what will happen tomorrow. What is your life? You are a mist that appears for a little while and then vanishes. Instead, you ought to say, 'If it is the Lord's will, we will live and do this and that.'"

Planning is not a bad thing. Planning can be good. It just needs to start with prayer and seeking God's guidance before embarking on plans of my own. Often times, the plans the Lord has for me are not the plans I would have chosen for myself. But I would rather follow the Lord's plans than my own plans. He never gets it wrong! When the plans I've made for myself turn out wrong, it may be the Lord's way of reminding me how very much I need him. And that he knows what is best for me. So, I will trust in the Lord's plans and talk to him before making my own. After all, when I make my own plans, it ends up with snoring, sighing, and a cot from 1912!

I think I'll stick with the Lord's plans. There probably aren't any squeaky cots in heaven!

PRAYER:

Thank you, Lord, for having a plan for my life. I
know you want what's best for me. Help me to seek
you before I embark on any plans of my own.

TWELVE

The Slow Demise of a Bottom Front Tooth

I had a root canal today. Yep, a root canal. Because I got hit in the mouth. By the back of a toddler's head. Two decades ago! I worked at a daycare, and a two-year-old was having a temper tantrum, which resulted in me taking a direct hit to my mouth. Turns out, getting smacked in the teeth with a human skull is kind of painful. There was blood. And tears. And my mouth was sore for a few days. But then it felt better. So, I went on with my life. But every so often, that bottom front tooth would bother me, like when I was drinking something cold or eating ice-cream. But it would only hurt for a moment, and then the pain would go away. So, I did what any responsible adult would do. I ignored it. It didn't hurt very often, so why should I bother going to the dentist to have it checked? Ignoring it worked just fine. Until it didn't.

One day, I noticed my bottom front tooth was becoming dis-colored. Just a little at first. And then a little more over time. Reluctantly, I decided it was time to go to the dentist. He looked at the offending tooth and proceeded to perform some kind of test. A horrible, medieval torture test! He touched the tooth with what looked like a cotton ball and said, "Tell me if it feels cold."

Umm . . . no. It wasn't cold. It was absolutely, painfully freezing! Bone chilling! That cotton ball must have been a snowball or an iceberg. Good grief! Oh man, did it hurt. After I peeled myself off the ceiling, I replied, "Umm, yeah. I guess you could say it's cold." And then that dentist actually said this was good news! It meant the tooth still had live nerves and wasn't completely dead. It didn't seem like good news to me. He told me I should have it checked out by a specialist. But I didn't. Hey, if the tooth was still alive that was good enough for me! It would be fine. Provided I didn't chew on any snowballs.

So, for a few more years, I lived with the tooth being a little sensitive once in a while. And becoming a little more discolored, which didn't bother me too much because it was a bottom tooth and therefore wasn't very visible. And for a few more years it was fine. Until it wasn't.

One day that tooth started hurting. And it didn't stop hurting. And then it started throbbing. And it didn't stop throbbing. The pain extended back into my jaw and ear. And it stayed that way. For days. Until I once again called the dentist. This time it was confirmed. The tooth had died slowly over the past twenty years due to the trauma caused by the blow to my mouth from the back of a toddler's head. And now the tooth was infected and that infection had spread to the jawbone. Hence the intense pain. Yuck! I was sent home with a painkiller, an antibiotic, and a referral for a root canal.

Well, wasn't this a lovely turn of events? I did not want to have a root canal. I had heard horror stories of root canals! Like intense pain and discomfort and flying bone fragments. And long needles inserted into your mouth and giant drills grinding your teeth. Nope, I did not want to have a root canal. But I also did not want to be in agonizing pain. So, ten days later, I walked into the dentist's office on shaky feet. With sweaty hands. And a dry mouth.

I sat down in that chair, closed my eyes, and waited for the torture to begin. The doctor was very nice as he explained the procedure. First came the needles filled with some kind of magical numbing juice. He said this would be the worst part. He did not lie. It was not pleasant. Plunging cold, sharp needles into tender gums under an infected tooth does not give you a warm, fuzzy feeling. In fact, it gives you the exact opposite of a warm, fuzzy feeling. Agony and anguish. Torment and suffering. Pain and more pain. But within moments, blissful numbness washed over my mouth. And we were ready to begin.

I closed my eyes. And prayed. And waited for horrible things to happen. But horrible things did not happen. Some discomfort happened. And I heard some unpleasant sounds. But the worst thing was that my upper lip kept getting squished between my teeth and the dentist's hand. Other than that, I felt nothing. And the drill wasn't nearly as loud as I thought it would be. The entire procedure was over in fifteen minutes, from start to finish! There was no torture. No intense pain. And no flying tooth fragments. Just like that, it was over. I drove home with a puffy lip, a partially numb tongue, and a feeling of immense relief.

But honestly, I also felt a little ashamed. Why had it taken me over twenty years to get that root canal? No, the tooth hadn't bothered me consistently for twenty years. But I knew it was a problem. I knew it would have to be taken care of sooner or later. I just chose later. Maybe out of fear over how much it would hurt, or how much it would cost. Thankfully, insurance covered the entire cost!

Putting off the procedure did not make my tooth better. In fact, it made it worse! How often do I hesitate to get rid of something in my life that is clearly not good for me? Why do I have so much trouble letting go of anger or hurt feelings? Or jealousy or bitterness? Why do I harbor unforgiveness in my heart?

Scripture instructs, "But now you must also rid yourselves of all such things as these: anger, rage, malice, slander, and filthy language from your lips" (Colossians 3:8). If we allow anger and unforgiveness to settle in our hearts, much like a damaged tooth, we can become infected. The longer we hold on to hurt and bitterness, the more the infection spreads, until it takes root and our hearts become hardened.

Letting go of the things that are not good is necessary for a healthy life. Not always easy, but necessary just the same. And, with God's help, it can be done! Just like a dentist performing a root canal, God can remove that infection. But first, you must go to him. Talk to him. Lay your burdens at his feet. Don't put it off! Believe me, it only makes things worse. If an infected heart hurts as much as an infected tooth, you do not want that!

Go to God! He can heal your heart. No drilling required.

PRAYER:

Lord, you are the Great Physician! Thank you for your healing touch in my life. Help me let go of things that harden my heart.

THIRTEEN

A Nose Hair Glistens in the Sun

Driving to church on Sunday morning can be an interesting experience. And by interesting, I mean hectic, stressful, and sometimes entertaining. It seems that someone always forgets something—a Bible, a coffee cup, or a sweater for those chilly mornings. And there is often a disappointed teenager in the back seat who is not happy with her hair. She can't get it to look the way she wants it to look, although I think it looks fine. But what do I know? I'm too old to understand teenage hair.

And the music selection! My husband and I like to listen to a classic country show that is only played on Sunday mornings. We love the old songs! One morning, we turned up the radio and sang along to the classic Jerry Reed hit, "When You're Hot, You're Hot." We sang it out loud and proud! We were thoroughly enjoying ourselves. Our daughters in the back seat, however, not so much. One of them actually said we were embarrassing! Now mind you, we were in our own car, with just our family, with the windows up! No one else could see or hear us. But according to our teenagers, this was still embarrassing behavior.

So, to respect their feelings, we did the only thing we could do.

We turned up the volume and sang a little louder! We may or may not have done a little dancing. Our daughters were not impressed, but we didn't care. We did, however, turn the radio down as we entered the church parking lot. The girls barely waited until the car stopped before jumping out and practically running into the building without us. You would've thought the devil was chasing them. I guess it was a good thing they were running into church.

One Sunday morning, I happened to glance at my husband in the driver's seat. I noticed something was out of place. A nose hair! I don't know how I saw that tiny little hair protruding from his nostrils. Usually, those little things just blend in with his mustache. But not this one! I saw it as plain as day. Maybe the sunlight hit it just right and reflected off the hair. Or maybe it was a divine occurrence. Maybe God was shining his light upon the offensive nose hair just so I would see it. Yes, I think that was the most logical explanation. God revealed it to me so it could be removed. I needed to tell my husband. I mean, God obviously wanted me to, right?

So, being the good wife that I am, I said, "Honey, you have a nose hair sticking out." His reaction was less than inspired. I believe his exact words were, "So what?" Really? Didn't he understand that I had just had a moment with God? So, I tried the direct approach. I believe I said something like, "No, seriously. It's gross. You need to remove it." After a little grumbling and asking for a specific location of the offending hair, he briefly glanced in the rearview mirror, pinched the little sucker between his thumb and forefinger, and yanked. Hard, apparently, because I heard him gasp. He said, "There. Did I get it?" Nope! He had not gotten it. So, he tried again. No luck! He tried a third time, but that little hair would not budge. It was cemented in place. His eyes were watering!

I decided I needed to step in and help him. After all, I was the one who started this thing in the first place. So, I searched my purse for a pair of tweezers. I couldn't find any. I did, however, find nail clippers. Hey, if we couldn't pluck the hair out by the root, maybe we could give it a trim! I held the clippers in the air and proclaimed, "Let's try these!" My husband was not as enthusiastic. For some reason, he didn't think it would work. I, however, thought using nail clippers to trim his nose hair while he was operating a moving vehicle was a fantastic idea! He obviously couldn't maneuver the clippers while driving, so I graciously volunteered to do the trimming myself. Again, he was less than thrilled.

I leaned closer to him, clippers poised for action and hand steady. Truth be told, I was kind of excited. I felt like a surgeon ready to operate. Or at least like I was playing the game "Operation." I hoped I had a steady hand. I didn't want to get zapped! I leaned in closer, positioned the clippers just right, and squeezed. Success! The hair was gone! But so was a chunk of my husband's nose! I heard him yell, "Ouch!" And then I saw the blood. To be fair, it was just a little blood. And the chunk of flesh I removed was more like a chunkette. Nonetheless, there was blood. But I counted it a victory because the hair was, in fact, gone! As my husband continued to wipe at his nose, I handed him a tissue and proclaimed, "I got it" just in case he didn't know. He did not share my enthusiasm. In fact, he kindly told me of his displeasure, declaring that he wished I would have just left that hair alone because it really hadn't looked that bad. Clearly, God and I felt differently!

Not surprisingly, my husband no longer lets me use sharp objects while in the car. I know it turned out to be a painful experience for him, but it was still absolutely necessary. Sometimes in life, we have to endure unpleasant circumstances. And usually, it's for our own good. Even if it is unpleasant, or painful, or downright miserable. But I have learned that pain is often necessary for growth. In Scripture, Jesus says, "I am the true vine, and my Father is the gardener. He cuts off every branch in me that bears no fruit, while every branch that does bear fruit he prunes so that it will be even more fruitful" (John 15:1–2).

My husband is an arborist. He knows that pruning dead branches from a tree is necessary for growth. It keeps the tree healthy, and allows the live branches to thrive. If the dead branches are not removed, the tree will become hazardous and will eventually begin to decay. Healthy branches need to be pruned routinely to ensure fruit production. Cutting back live branches allows even more fruit to grow. God prunes our dead branches in order to keep us healthy. He wants us to grow and thrive! And sometimes he prunes our healthy branches to allow us to grow even more.

But just like that nose hair mishap, pruning can be painful, yet necessary! That short temper I have when I snap at my children? Dead branch! That false sense of pride I feel when I think I am right and my husband is so obviously wrong? Dead branch! Letting fear take over and neglecting to trust that God is in control of my life? Dead branch! I don't want to carry around dead branches. I want the Master Gardener, God himself, to prune them. I want to be a happy, healthy fruit-producing tree! Even if it means enduring a little pain. Or maybe a lot of pain. Because in the end, I know that is what's best for me. And I know that God knows what he is doing. He is the Master Gardener. I trust him to trim my branches.

No nail clippers needed!

PRAYER:

God, you are the Master Gardener! Thank you
for pruning my branches so I can grow. I trust
you to know what is best for my life.

FOURTEEN

Little Sisters Make Good Bathroom Buddies

When I was a kid, I loved going to visit my grandparents' house. It was originally an old one-room schoolhouse that was later converted into a church social hall. My grandparents bought the building in 1960 and turned it into their home. I just loved that place. It seemed so magical and mysterious.

From the front porch, there was a view of rolling farm fields with beautiful mountains in the distance. I loved to sit on the porch swing on a sunny day and pretend I was flying an airplane.

The living room had a high ceiling lined with fancy tiles. A little window looked out the back of the house onto a farm field. I used to imagine a child from the old one-room schoolhouse days sitting at a desk, staring out the window, dreaming about playing in that field on a warm spring day. Just off the living room was a hallway that led to the bedrooms. The walls were covered in a funky, gold-patterned wallpaper that my grandma put up herself.

There were three bedrooms at the back of the house. My mother's old bedroom had an accordion-style door and a double bed where my sisters and I would sleep when we stayed overnight. My grandparents' bedroom had a slightly warped hardwood floor. An old-timey picture of my great-great-grandparents hung on the wall. I loved to look at that picture. The third room was my uncle's old bedroom. This room had a window with a view of the cemetery that was just a stone's throw across an old farm lane. I loved looking out that window—in the daytime. But once nightfall came, I would not set foot in that room! The cemetery was scary in the dark!

The kitchen was my favorite room in the house. It was long and narrow and really didn't have much space. But it always smelled like turkey and stuffing and mashed potatoes and coconut cake. When we had Christmas dinner, all the kids had to sit between the table and the wall. We would squeeze into our chairs first, because once the adults sat down, there was no way to get in or out!

The one room in the house I didn't especially love was the bathroom. Actually, I didn't like it at all because it was located in the basement. And when I say basement, I do not mean finished lower-level family room. No, I'm talking concrete floor, stone walls, dark, musty basement! With lots of boxes. And no windows. A set of steep wooden stairs led to the basement. The bathroom was just steps away from the landing. It was a dark room, with just a toilet, a tub, and a sink. No window. Right outside the bathroom door stood the well pump. From the time the toilet was flushed, you had all of five seconds before the pump kicked on. And it was loud! I'm talking deafening! I was scared of that thing. My sister was scared of that thing.

Needless to say, I did not like to go to the bathroom alone. My little sister did not like to go to the bathroom alone. So, we buddied up and went together. We would hold hands and brave the rickety steps that led to the dark depths of the cellar. Once inside the bathroom, we quickly tended to our business. After we finished, we would both wash our hands. One of us would turn out the light and open the door, while the other sister took her place by the toilet.

And on the count of three, she would flush. And then we ran, hands over our ears, as fast as our little legs would carry us! Like we were being chased by a bear. Or like the Road Runner fleeing from Wile E. Coyote. We didn't stop until we reached the top of the stairs.

The funny thing was that on our way down the steps, my sister and I worked hand-in-hand. Literally. We helped each other descend the stairs. We worked together to flush the toilet. But once that pump kicked on, it was every sister for herself! We would both run as fast as we could. But I was older, and taller, and faster. Once I started up those stairs, I kept running without a single backward glance. With no concern for my little sister. Hey, my life was at stake. Or at least my ears. I fell more than once and bruised my shins while sprinting up those steep steps. I'm guessing my sister fell more than once, too. But if she did, I never knew. My eyes were focused on the door to the hallway at the top of the stairs. She may have fallen down the steps completely for all I knew. But she always made it to the top, about ten seconds after me. I waited for her on the other side of the basement door. Where it was safe.

When I was a teenager, my grandparents converted a large hall closet on the main floor into a brand-new bathroom. It was awesome! No more trips into the depths of the dark basement. No more going to the bathroom with my little sister. No more running for my life from the ear-splitting noise of the well pump. Ironically, even when you flushed the toilet in the new upstairs bathroom, you could still hear the well pump kick on. But it was not as loud. And I was not as scared.

As I look back on those days, I have fond memories of those trips down the basement steps. Oh, I didn't enjoy it at the time. But now I can appreciate those childhood memories. Holding my sister's hand as we carefully trudged down those steep stairs. Working together to turn out the light and flush the toilet. Having someone I could count on to brave that scary noise with!

We read in Ecclesiastes that "two are better than one, because they have a good return for their labor: If either of them falls down, one can help the other up. But pity anyone who falls and has no one to help them up" (Ecclesiastes 4:9–10).

Okay, to be fair, I never stopped to help my sister up! But I was young. And scared. I would like to think that if she fell today, I would stop to help her up. Right after I finished laughing! I'm kidding, of course. I would help her up before I finished laughing. But aside from that falling down part, this verse totally applies!

Everyone needs a friend. Someone to count on. Someone to support you and comfort you and cheer you on. Someone to hold your hand when life gets scary. Someone who will walk beside you and not run ahead of you to save herself from the deafening noise of a well pump. Because two are better than one. And life is easier with the help of a friend.

And basements are not as scary with your little sister by your side.

PRAYER:

Lord, you know the value and importance of friendship.
Thank you for blessing me with friends. Help me to be
a blessing to the friends you've placed in my life.

FIFTEEN

Coffee Tastes Better in a Quiet House

It was one of those mornings. The kind when you feel like you have no time to yourself. No place to call your own. Nowhere to hide when you just want five minutes of peace. The kind of Sunday morning that actually starts on Saturday!

Saturday night, 10:00 p.m. My seventeen-year-old daughter asked if she could borrow a shirt and sweater to wear to church the following morning. The shirt was super cute and I had worn it to church a few weeks earlier, so I wasn't planning to wear it the next day. Plus, I thought it was pretty cool that my teenage daughter wanted to borrow my clothes. I must be trendy. Or hip. Or something. So, no problem, I let her borrow the shirt. But the blue sweater . . . I was actually planning to wear that! I tried steering her toward a pink sweater. Or a white one. But no, she preferred the blue. Being the nice mother that I am, I let her have the blue one and decided I would wear the black one. Although I may or may not have had a slight attitude about giving up the blue sweater.

Fast forward to Sunday morning. I got up at 6:30 (okay, closer to 7:00), took a shower, got dressed, and made a pot of coffee. My oldest daughter left for church. She had to be there early (which was why she chose her outfit the night before). She's the worship leader. Pretty cool, huh? My husband went for a run. My youngest daughter went outside to feed the goats. I finally had a few minutes to myself. I was just sitting down to drink my coffee and play a little Candy Crush on my phone when my husband returned from his run, sweaty and ready for a shower. Off he went to the bathroom. Good. I was alone once again! Time to enjoy my coffee. I had taken only two sips (maybe three) when my youngest daughter came back in the house, walked into the kitchen, and proceeded to make a bagel. Then she promptly walked into the living room, bagel in hand, and plopped down on the couch right beside me! Umm, really? Listen, I love my family. But listening to my daughter eat her breakfast did not fit into my plan of relaxation. So, I politely (or not so much) excused myself and headed to my bedroom, coffee cup in hand, hoping to find a little peace and quiet. Alone. But as I entered the room, I saw my husband was still in our bathroom, with the door open, just about to step in the shower. Lovely! This was not what I had in mind for pleasant relaxation. I turned around and made a hasty retreat from the bedroom. I headed to the office at the other end of the hall. I sat down at the desk, finally sipped my coffee, and got to work trying to beat Level 523. Ahh! It looked like I had finally found a quiet place. Or maybe not. I was in the room all of twenty-three seconds when our beagle began scratching at the door. Good grief!

And that was the moment I lost it. I began shouting, "Seriously?! All I want is five minutes to myself! Is this too much to ask? I think not! I have no place to myself! I have no peace and quiet in this house! I can't sit on the couch! I can't go in my own bedroom! I can't even wear my own sweater! And now the dog won't leave me alone!"

And that was the end of my rant. I don't know why I bothered yelling. It did no good. No one was listening to me. So, I gave up.

My coffee was cold, anyway. My five minutes of peace were spent wandering around the house like the Hebrew children searching for the Promised Land.

Didn't I deserve five minutes alone? Five minutes of uninterrupted quiet, with no talking or chewing or scratching? Or sweater borrowing! Just five minutes to enjoy my coffee.

Well, it didn't happen. I found no time for myself that particular Sunday morning. No peace and quiet. No perfect resting place.

Sometimes my search seems so futile. Because maybe what I'm searching for isn't an actual, physical place. Maybe finding rest is less about where I am and more about who I'm with. Maybe it's more about *who* I run to than *where* I run to.

In Matthew 11:28, Jesus says, "Come to me, all you who are weary and burdened, and I will give you rest." True rest can only be found in running to God. Talking with him. Dwelling in his presence. Resting in his arms. Psalm 62:1 says, "Truly my soul finds rest in God; my salvation comes from him."

That is where my soul finds rest. But not just for five minutes. God offers peace that will last a lifetime. In fact, an eternity! He offers peace that can't be found anywhere else.

Oh, I'm sure I'll still occasionally wander through my house searching for that elusive peace and quiet. But if I search for the peace that only God can give, if I seek him out when I need rest, I will be far less likely to wander aimlessly through the wilderness looking for a place to hide.

Or a quiet place to drink my coffee!

PRAYER:

Lord, thank you for offering me the peace only you
can provide. May I find rest in you alone.

SIXTEEN

The Big Backside and the Flowered Muumuu

When I was seven months pregnant with my youngest daughter, I began having contractions. This was obviously too early to be having contractions, so I was sent to the hospital. I had some tests that determined the contractions were the beginning of pre-term labor, and therefore needed to be stopped. I was given medication and an IV to push fluids. And I had to drink water. Lots and lots of water. Approximately 1,000 gallons of water. Which resulted in ninety-three trips to the bathroom to dispose of that water. But it did the trick and stopped the contractions. I was sent home with orders for strict bedrest for one month. No heavy lifting, no climbing stairs, no exercise (no problem), and lots of rest for four weeks. My first thoughts were, *How in the world am I going to handle four weeks of bedrest? I have a two-year-old daughter to take care of. Plus, a house to keep in order. Not to mention a husband to keep happy!* But I knew bedrest was best for the baby, and for myself. So, I relented.

My husband was a great help, and thankfully our daughter could do lots of things for herself. So, I rested, as if I had a choice. I laid on the couch. And drank gallons of water. And made forty-seven trips to the bathroom per day. Which seemed counterproductive to the bedrest. It should really be called bathroom rest, because I certainly spent more time in the bathroom than in bed. Or resting. I was tired. Even with all the rest I was getting. I felt lazy and useless. And I was huge! Like a beached whale. I wore pajamas all day long. I wore no make-up. What was the point? I wasn't allowed to leave the house! I felt like a gigantic, unattractive whale in maternity pajama pants!

But I survived, and four weeks later I was allowed off bedrest. If I went into labor at thirty-six weeks, the baby would be just fine. I did not go into labor at thirty-six weeks. In fact, the bedrest worked a little too well, because the baby came two days late!

My first day off bedrest was Easter Sunday. I was so excited! Hooray! I had the perfect reason to look pretty and wear make-up and a lovely Easter dress. The problem was the only dress I had that fit was a giant, yellow-flowered muumuu. Okay, it wasn't actually a muumuu. But it was big. And when I put it on, I looked like I was wearing a tent. A gigantic, yellow, muumuu maternity tent. It was Easter and I wanted to go to church. But my self-confidence had taken a hit. A month of bedrest will do that to you!

Even with my hair styled, my face made up, and wearing a frilly dress, I still felt unattractive. I looked in a full-length mirror to assess the situation. The mirror confirmed my suspicions. Yep, my dress looked like a muumuu, but it was my only choice. I would just have to deal with it. My belly was enormous, but at eight months pregnant, there was no hiding it. No problem. I could accept the size of my belly. What really bothered me was my backside. It was huge! I thought it looked massive in the mirror. Maybe it was the light. Or the angle. I shifted my position and looked again. Nope. That didn't help. There was no getting around it. My backside was enormous. But maybe I was just being overly sensitive. You know, hormones and all.

So, I decided to ask my husband. Yep, you heard that right. I sought advice from my husband on the appearance of my giant, pregnant body. Specifically, my backside. What was I thinking? Must have been the hormones. I found my husband in the kitchen, looking oh-so-handsome in his dressy church pants and festive Easter tie. I marched right up to him and asked, "Honey, does my butt look big?" He looked at me with those brilliant blue eyes, gave me a dashing smile and said, "It has to be big. If it wasn't, you'd fall forward and topple over. Your butt is a counterbalance for your belly."

Umm . . . Say what now? Had I heard him correctly? Did he actually say my butt was big? Maybe my hormones were messing with my hearing. It was the hormones, right? Or could it be the muumuu? Maybe he was hypnotized by the yellow-flowered muumuu and had no control over what he was saying. But he was smiling. He looked happy. As if he were pleased with himself. Like he had just won Jeopardy. "I'll take insensitive things to say to your pregnant wife for $800, Alex."

No, there was no mistake. He had actually said it. And I had actually heard it. I stared at him in shock. And then I cried. And then I got mad. I don't remember for sure, but I probably threw something at him. Now let me just say that my husband is very loving and kind. He treats me very well. He took care of me when I was on bedrest. He made dinner, and washed dishes, and brought me seventy-five gallons of water a day. He did laundry and took care of our daughter. He even made her birthday cake. He was wonderful and I loved him. But in that moment, I was not too fond of him. My feelings were hurt. I wanted to smack him. With a frying pan. A cast iron frying pan! But he spoke the truth. I was, in fact, huge. In the front, and in the back!

But just because it was true did not mean it was meant to be spoken. Don't get me wrong, I believe in honesty. But that does not mean every thought that pops into my head should come out of my mouth. Truth or not. Proverbs 17:27 says, "The one who has knowledge uses words with restraint." Restraint. In other words, hold your tongue. Weigh your words before you speak them. Not every word needs to be spoken. I know this firsthand. I am usually the one who has trouble holding my tongue, not my husband. I still think the muumuu affected his sanity.

I often catch myself saying something I shouldn't say. The trouble is, I don't always catch it until after it comes out of my mouth. Words are very powerful. They should be used to encourage others. To build them up, not tear them down. Scripture says, "Therefore encourage one another and build each other up" (1 Thessalonians 5:11). This can be a difficult thing to do. But keeping a tight rein on your tongue and thinking before you speak can make it a little easier. There is wisdom in knowing that sometimes, some things are better left unsaid. Even if they are true. And silence is always the best choice when it comes to the size of your pregnant wife's backside. After all, Proverbs 21:23 says, "Those who guard their mouths and their tongues keep themselves from calamity." Like a frying pan alongside your head. A cast iron one!

PRAYER:

Thank you, Father, for the gift of words! Give me wisdom
to know when to speak and when to remain silent. May
my words be an encouragement to someone today.

SEVENTEEN

Warning! Tilt-A-Whirl: Proceed with Caution

Have you ever had vertigo? Well, I have. And let me tell you, it is not fun at all! It is an intense spinning sensation, far worse than regular dizziness. It feels like you are spinning, twisting, and falling through the air, like one of those astronauts on a Tang commercial from the 1960s. Except when your feet hit the ground, you are not rewarded with an orange drink. Nope, you get a heaping helping of nausea, and a handful of drenching sweats. Sounds delightful, doesn't it?

Well, that is just what happened to me one night. I am a side-sleeper by nature. I usually sleep on my right side, but at times I will choose my left. Sometimes in my sleep, unbeknownst to me, I roll from one side to the other. I guess my brain can't decide which side it likes more.

One night, in the midst of turning from my right to my left side, BAM! That's when it hit! Instant vertigo! I felt like I was falling off a roller coaster. And not one of those good, safe rollercoasters at a reputable amusement park. I'm talking about the Tilt-A-Whirl that's being run by the nearly toothless guy at the Podunk carnival.

You know, the one with a mullet, whose name is probably Bubba. Or Billy Bob.

Yep, I was spinning out of control, helplessly falling through the air, certain I would hit the ground. If only I could get Billy Bob Bubba to stop the ride! I wanted to get off! But no, it kept twirling and whirling with no end in sight. And that's when my stomach started twirling and whirling. I somehow managed to stop the Tilt-A-Whirl long enough to sit up on the edge of the bed. Goodness knows Bubba was no help at all!

After teetering my way to the bathroom, I was rewarded with dripping sweat, followed by more spinning. I managed to call for my husband who gallantly, though groggily, came to my rescue.

The next few hours were a blur of dizziness and nausea and sweating and tears. And prayers—my husband's prayers for my health and speedy recovery, along with my own prayers of "Dear Lord, please make it stop!" And finally, in the wee hours of the morning, it stopped. Well, mostly, anyway.

Having vertigo is a completely terrifying feeling. You have no control over what is happening. You desperately want it to stop. And trust me, it is a horrible feeling knowing that in that moment, Billy Bob has more control over your life than you do!

Vertigo is not something I brought upon myself. But what about those other things in my life that I desperately try to control? Like my daughter graduating from high school and going to college literally halfway around the world? Okay, maybe it's only ten hours away, but whatever. It feels like it's halfway around the world.

Or sending my baby (okay, not literally my baby; she's fifteen, but whatever) halfway across the country to overnight church camp for an entire week! Okay, so it's only an hour away, but it feels like it's halfway across the country. Or maybe it's sickness. Or the death of a loved one. Oh, how I cried when my grandfather passed away!

These are things I cannot control. I do not have ultimate control over my life. But thank the Lord that Billy Bob Bubba doesn't have control of it either! The good Lord has control. He always has and he always will! He is the master roller-coaster operator. If I keep my eyes on him, I will not fall.

When the disciples saw Jesus walking on the water, they were terrified! In Matthew 14:27, Jesus said to them, "Take courage! It is I. Don't be afraid." But that wasn't good enough for Peter. He didn't believe it was really Jesus walking on that water. He wanted proof. So, in verse 29, Jesus told Peter to come to him. Peter got out of the boat and walked on the water toward Jesus. But as soon as he saw the wind and the waves, he became afraid. He took his eyes off Jesus, and he began to sink! Verse 31 says that Jesus immediately reached out his hand and caught Peter. "You of little faith," he said. "Why did you doubt?"

Wow! Jesus had complete control over the storm. When Peter's eyes were firmly fixed on Jesus, he was able to do the impossible. He walked on water! But the very moment Peter took his eyes off Jesus and tried to take back control, he began to sink.

And that is exactly what vertigo feels like. Out-of-control sinking! In those moments when I try to take complete control of my own life, that is when I really lose control. That is when vertigo sets in. And that is when I sink.

As much as I would like to, I can't control every aspect of my life. I can't control the aging and maturing process of my children. I can't keep them at home with me forever, though I wish I could! But what I can do is give that control over to God, because it's really his anyway. If I keep my eyes fixed on him, he will help me through the vertigo. Because I certainly do not want to ride on that Tilt-A-Whirl ever again! Trust me, God is a far better ride operator than Billy Bob Bubba ever could be!

PRAYER:

Oh God, you are sovereign and have control over all things! Thank you for your loving protection over my life. Help me trust you in those moments when my life feels like it's spinning out of control.

EIGHTEEN

Chubby Bunny

Have you ever played the game, "Chubby Bunny?" You know the one. It's the game where you put a marshmallow in your mouth and then say the words, "Chubby Bunny." Then you shove another marshmallow in and say it again. You keep adding one marshmallow at a time, saying "Chubby Bunny" after each addition, until you just can't fit another fluffy marshmallow into your mouth. The goal is to see how may marshmallows you can fit in your face while still being able to say the words, "Chubby Bunny."

What is the point of this game? I have no idea! It's just fun, and was probably invented by a bunch of twelve-year-old boys. I must admit I enjoyed playing this game as a kid. Well, let me be clear. I did not enjoy overloading my own mouth with marshmallows. But I loved watching my friends overload theirs! It was hilarious! Seeing their cheeks puffed up like a squirrel storing nuts for the winter. Watching drool ooze out of the corners of their mouths once the marshmallows began to dissolve. Listening to them attempt to say "Chubby Bunny," then trying desperately not to gag because they were laughing so hard they couldn't breathe. That stuff is hysterical when you're eleven years old. Or sixteen years old, if you're a boy.

Just ask my husband. He was the "Chubby Bunny" champion of his high school. Seriously. He got a certificate and everything! He and his friends liked to play "Chubby Bunny" at lunch. Somehow, my husband defeated all the other sixteen-year-old boys. I guess he had a big mouth, or stretchy cheeks, or maybe an extreme love for marshmallows. The day he became champion, he actually stuffed twenty-seven marshmallows in his mouth. Not mini marshmallows, either. Nope, these were full-sized! He then proceeded to say "Chubby Bunny" in a somewhat muffled, but still audible voice, as per the rules.

Sticky marshmallow dripped from the corners of his mouth and spilled onto his chin. His buddies must have found this quite amusing, because they howled in laughter, which triggered a guffaw from my husband, which inevitably sent a mouthful of partially dissolved, slimy white marshmallows flying across the cafeteria. The goo ultimately landed on the floor, two nearby tables, the lunch tray of one unlucky kid, and in the hair of a few innocent bystanders. And that is how my husband became the reigning "Chubby Bunny" champion of his high school, and—as he would have you believe—also a living legend! And now I am married to him! Oh, I'm one lucky girl!

The image of a teenage boy with twenty-seven marshmallows crammed into his mouth sure paints a funny picture. But it also serves as a good reminder of how we should live our lives. Okay, stay with me here. Marshmallows are a tasty treat that many people enjoy. But most people don't stuff them in their mouths until they are quite literally spilling out!

But that's exactly what we should be doing—except not with marshmallows. Instead, with the Word of God. We should be reading the Bible, memorizing Scripture, and living out the contents of the pages, from Genesis to Revelation. Hiding God's Word in our hearts. Filling our lives and hearts and minds so full of God's Word that we literally cannot contain it!

Scripture reminds us, "A good man brings good things out of the good stored up in his heart, and an evil man brings evil things out of the evil stored up in his heart. For the mouth speaks what the heart is full of" (Luke 6:45).

What is my heart full of? Is it overflowing with good, evil, or marshmallows?

Oh, I hope it's filled with good things! It should be my desire to cram my heart so full of God's Word that I simply cannot contain it. God's love should be oozing out of me like dissolving marshmallows. But that won't happen if I eat only one marshmallow at a time, or no marshmallows at all! How many times do I read only one Bible verse, or a quick devotional, just to say I've done it? Just to check it off my list.

I need to fill my life with an abundance of God's Word. I should be consuming it with as much enthusiasm as a kid playing "Chubby Bunny." My goal should be to become the reigning "Chubby Bunny" champion. But not with marshmallows. With the true and living Word of God.

Give it a try. Read God's words. Then read some more. I promise, there is room in your heart for an unlimited amount of God's Word.

I can't say the same for marshmallows.

PRAYER:

Dear Lord, your Word is a lamp for my feet and a light
for my path (Psalm 119:105). May I crave the truth of
your Word as much as marshmallows—so much so that it
overflows from my heart and oozes out of my mouth.

NINETEEN

Pack Your Suitcase, But Leave Room for God

My family and I recently returned from vacation. A relaxing one-week stay in the breathtaking mountains of east Tennessee. We had a very nice time. But vacations can be a lot of work. Especially for the moms! It all starts with planning. We booked our cabin three months in advance. And for three months, we looked forward to our trip. No work. No alarm clocks. No timeline. Just our entire family. Together. Having fun.

We talked about what activities we wanted to do. We talked about what restaurants we wanted to eat at. We even talked about what rides we wanted to go on at the amusement park. (Or not. I don't do roller coasters.) We started a countdown a few weeks before vacation began. We were very much looking forward to our week in the mountains. Each day was one day closer! Our excitement grew until finally, the big day arrived! Although, waking up at 4:30 in the morning wasn't the best way to start the day. Everyone was a little tired. And grumpy. But we all got over it soon enough. After all, this was the day we had waited for! Looking forward to a vacation is half the fun! But preparing for a vacation is not quite as much fun.

I do practically all the vacation preparation for my family. I start making lists at least two weeks before the big day. Clothing. What outfits do I need to pack for everyone? How many pairs of shorts? How many shirts? Maybe I should pack something a little nicer in case we go someplace fancy. (By the way, this never happens.) And everyone needs a swimsuit for tubing on the river. So, I packed a swimsuit for everyone. Except myself. I forgot my swimsuit. (Side note: My husband offered to buy me one of those flimsy little swimsuits from the souvenir store. He thought it was a lovely idea. Me, not so much. I did not buy one of those cheap little things. I just wore shorts and a t-shirt instead.) Once the clothes were packed, I focused on toiletries. Shampoo for the girls, a plethora of facial products, toothbrushes, nail clippers, soap, lotion, and toilet paper. Yes, toilet paper. I always bring my own. I like to use the super-soft, ultra-thick brand. The kind they provide for you at the rental is always scratchy. And thin. Seriously, you can see through it. I was not going to spend a week using subpar toilet paper. Call me a snob, that's okay. But my hiney sure was happy!

Besides packing for the people, I also have to make arrangements for the animals. We have chickens and goats that need to be fed and watered daily. Thankfully, our neighbor kindly offered to look after them. And then there's the dog. She is an old, blind, diabetic beagle who is very sweetly disposed, but needs special attention. She has to eat the same amount of food at the same time twice daily and then receive an insulin injection after each feeding. We could not leave her with just anyone. So, Grandma kindly offered to watch her. But to make things easier, I prefilled each syringe with the proper amount of insulin. Two syringes per day for seven days. I also measured out and individually bagged her food. Two bags per day for seven days. Plus a few extra, just in case. And then there's all the dog paraphernalia: bed, leash, kennel, and pee pads. Yes, pee pads! She is old and diabetic and sometimes has accidents.

Once the dog was taken care of, there were still fifty million other things to do or pack—give or take a few million. And I am the one who has to pack them, because I am the mother and, apparently, it's my job! But that's okay. I want my family to have a fantastic vacation! And if that means making sure to pack the fifteen-year-old's teal blue shirt and not the greenish-blue one, then that is what I'll do. Or packing the squishy memory foam flip-flops for the seventeen-year-old that she didn't even remember she owned so her feet would be comfortable all week, I'm glad to do it! Or packing, well, everything, for my husband, including all the things he needs, even though he thinks he only needs two t-shirts for seven days. It's okay, I packed at least seven. Because I love him. I love all of them. And I want them to have a wonderful vacation! And we did, in fact, have a wonderful vacation!

Looking forward to and preparing for a vacation is a fine thing. It's necessary. But I can't help thinking, do I look forward to spending time with God as much as I look forward to spending a week in the mountains? Am I as excited to read my Bible as I am to get on that roller coaster? Okay, bad example. I don't do roller coasters. But my family does, so you get what I mean. I should be eager to spend time with God. Scripture says, "And without faith it is impossible to please God, because anyone who comes to him must believe that he exists and that he rewards those who earnestly seek him" (Hebrews 11:6). Do I earnestly seek the Lord every day? What does earnestly mean, anyway? To earnestly seek the Lord is to do so with sincere and intense conviction. Wow! Sincere and intense. That's, well . . . intense! Do I run after the Lord like a hungry kid running after the ice cream truck on a hot summer day? Now that's intense! And also, a really good idea! I should be looking forward to my time with God, resting in his presence, and growing in the knowledge of his truth.

Preparing your heart to spend time with the Lord is something that shouldn't be overlooked. It is so easy to become distracted by so many things: cell phones, social media, email, TV, music, and even relationships with other people. Preparing your heart to spend time with the Lord begins with eliminating—or at the very least, resisting—distractions. Turn off the TV, social media, and your cell phone. Resist the urge to check off another item on that to-do list. Hold off on checking your email. All of these things serve a purpose, but can also be great distractions. Turn them off and be intentional about spending time with God. Preparing to spend time with God looks less like packing for vacation, and more like unpacking, decluttering, and getting back to basics.

Once the distractions have been removed, you'll have room to fill your heart with the truth of God's Word. A heart overflowing with the Word of God is more valuable than a well-packed suitcase. Truly, there is no greater joy than spending time with the Lord.

Not a fun-filled family vacation. Not a week off work. And definitely not a ride on a roller coaster!

PRAYER:

Dear Lord, I am thankful for your presence in my life. I look forward to spending time with you. Help me to be intentional in making time to spend with you each day.

TWENTY

Patience on Sale, Aisle 3

I do my grocery shopping on Thursday mornings. I like to arrive at the store early, before it gets crowded and chaotic and filled with crazies. I usually navigate through the aisles without too much difficulty. Of course, sometimes, there are little annoyances that jump in my way. Like the lady who pushes her cart straight down the middle of the aisle, leaving absolutely no room to pass on the right or the left! Or the screaming toddler, running around with a lollipop dangling from his sticky mouth, knocking cereal boxes onto the floor, leaving no room to pass, on the right or the left! But, for the most part, if I arrive early enough, I can make it through the store and to the checkout in a decent amount of time.

On one particular Thursday, I had plans to meet my husband and some friends for breakfast at a local restaurant at 9:30. I decided to squeeze in my shopping trip before our breakfast outing. As I made my way to the front of the store, I found only one checkout line open! Only one! There are twenty-four registers and only one was open. Well, the 20 Items or Less Express Lane was open, but I easily had fifty-two items in my cart. The self-checkout registers were open, but again, fifty-two items! I did not want to go down that route. So, I reluctantly pushed my cart to the one and only register available to me. There were three ladies in front of me. I checked the time: 8:51. *No problem.* The ladies in front of me did not have too many items, and the first lady was almost done. *I should be checked out and on my way to breakfast in no time!* I thought I was in good shape. I didn't mind waiting for a few minutes, and I had plenty of time before I needed to leave the store. But, five minutes passed and the line stood still. I didn't move forward one inch! I glanced behind me and found that three more people had joined the line. I turned back around and made eye contact with the older lady in front of me. She smiled and shrugged and said, "Hurry up and wait, right?" I smiled and said something witty in reply. And then I continued to wait.

Lady #1 finally paid and pushed her cart away. Great! Lady #2 began to check out and Lady #3 started placing her items on the conveyor belt. Fantastic! Things were finally moving! Until they weren't. It seemed Lady #2 had a question about every one of her items. And then the scanner thingy beeped and the cashier punched a code into the register. Oh no! Not that! Everything came to a screeching halt while we waited for the supervisor to come fix whatever it was that went wrong. I glanced at the clock again: 9:07. At this rate I would never make it to breakfast on time. As I waited— rather impatiently—my irritation grew. I was hot. I was hungry. And I had to go to the bathroom! I tried to keep the comments bouncing around in my head to myself, but somehow the words, "Good grief, this is ridiculous!" slipped right out of my mouth! The lady behind me must have heard, because she began explaining that she was too tired from working a twelve-hour shift to even care what was happening. She just wanted to go home and go to bed!

Finally, the situation with Lady #2 was resolved, and she left the checkout line. As the cashier began scanning the items for Lady #3, I placed my groceries on the conveyor belt. I checked the time: 9:14.

Okay, if I could get out the door in the next five minutes, I might just make it to the restaurant on time. Things were looking up.

And then it happened. Lady #3 presented a coupon to the cashier. She scanned it, and it didn't work. The cashier told her it wasn't valid. She had the wrong kind of shampoo. Lady #3 assured her it was not the wrong kind of shampoo, and she wanted her dollar off! And then they both proceeded to search through every single bag until they found that stinking bottle of shampoo. I am not kidding. Every. Single. Bag. At this point, I was beyond irritated. I was angry. And hungry. And I still had to go to the bathroom! I must have lost control of my mouth, because I suddenly blurted out, "Good grief. Forget the coupon. I'll just give her a dollar!" Thankfully, I hadn't said it very loudly, because the lady behind me was the only one who seemed to notice. I was so flustered that I missed what happened with the coupon. But I'm fairly certain Lady #3 received her dollar off, because she walked away with a smile on her face. A gigantic one-dollar smile!

And then, finally, after what felt like an eternity, it was my turn. I checked the time: 9:20. There was no chance I would make it to the restaurant on time. But, to the cashier's credit, she managed to get me through her line in a record amount of time. Probably because I didn't have any coupons. I walked out the door at precisely 9:25, after thirty-four minutes of standing in line! I all but ran out of the store, flung the groceries into my car, and drove slightly faster than I should have to the restaurant. I arrived seven minutes late—but I still got there before my friends! Good grief! All that irritation and aggravation was for nothing!

Why is waiting so difficult? In my defense, I really should not have had to wait thirty-four minutes in line at the grocery store. It was an annoying and inconvenient situation. But waiting takes patience. And apparently, I am in short supply of patience.

Patience is really what's at the heart of waiting.

I did not want to wait such a long time in a place where I did not want to be while I was tired and hungry (and had to go to the bathroom). I let my irritation take control. Which, in reality, made the situation worse. Listen, I don't think there is anything I could've done to get out of that line faster. I had no control of the situation. I could not change my circumstance. But I could've exercised a little patience, which would have changed my attitude.

What if, instead of becoming irritated and muttering not-so-nice things under my breath, I decided to speak kind words? What if I had struck up a conversation with the lady behind me who had worked a twelve-hour shift? Maybe I could have offered her a word of encouragement. Or at the very least, a pleasant distraction from the annoying situation we both found ourselves in.

What if I had offered to help the coupon lady find her bottle of shampoo instead of offering a bribe in an effort to make the line move faster? That probably would have been a better use of my time. But that day, in the checkout line, I chose frustration over patience. And I may have missed an opportunity to be a blessing to someone else.

Psalm 37:7 says, "Be still before the LORD and wait patiently for him." And let me tell you, sometimes it's hard. Hard to be still. Hard to wait. And definitely hard to wait patiently.

But there it is, in the Word. Be still. Wait patiently. No matter the circumstances. Even when you're tired. Even when you're hungry.

And especially when you're in line at the grocery store.

PRAYER:

Lord, waiting is so difficult. Help me to be patient,
especially in trying situations. Thank you for providing
opportunities to be a blessing to others. Open my
eyes so I don't miss those opportunities.

TWENTY-ONE

Climbing a Mountain Brings Out the Sweat in Me

When my husband and I were dating, we loved to go hiking. We enjoyed exploring the mountains and spending time in the woods. Now, we still love to be in the woods. And he still likes to hike. Especially when he's on the trail of a deer. And I still like to be outside. But I now do more walking than actual hiking. But twenty-five years ago, when we were young, we loved to hike!

One sunny fall afternoon, we drove up into the mountains on an old rocky road and found a beautiful trail. We went prepared with a backpack stocked with water bottles, snacks, a sweatshirt, a Bible, and a book of Robert Frost poems. Robert Frost is my favorite! We started out on a trail that steadily slanted down a steep hill. Eventually, we came to the perfect place to stop and view the magnificent mountains. We sat down and snuggled close together. Birds sang, the sun shone down, and the gentle breeze blew as we gazed into each other's eyes and enjoyed the peace and stillness of the afternoon. Okay, it may not have been that magical, but that's how I choose to remember it! We talked and read the Bible and Robert Frost and thoroughly enjoyed our time together.

Until it was time to go! Remember when I said we hiked down a steep trail? Well, what comes down must go up. Or something like that. I took one look at the nearly-vertical trail ahead and immediately felt uneasy. This path looked treacherous. It looked like I was going to have to exert much effort. It looked like I was going to sweat. A lot! And I did not want to get all sweaty in front of my super-cute future husband. He was Mr. Physical Fitness. This climb would be no problem for him! By nature, I am not the most positive person. I'm not necessarily negative. I'd say I'm realistic. And realistically, I knew there was no way I was getting up the side of that mountain without some serious huffing and puffing. And I did not want to turn into the Big Bad Wolf! Not in front of my physically fit, oh-so-handsome boyfriend. But, being young and in love, and wanting to please my man, I smiled, reached for his hand, inwardly groaned, and started up that trail.

At first, I was fine. For about four minutes. Then I started to slow down, and breathe heavily, and then slow down some more. I wanted to stop. And sit. And catch my breath. But I kept walking. Well, plodding, really. And sweating. And smiling at my super-cute boyfriend. He glanced in my direction. I'm sure he noticed my distress. And I know he saw me sweating. He couldn't miss it. Droplets were dripping off my forehead. I must have looked stunning. But then my sweetie did a strange thing. He stopped walking and looked at me. I gazed upon his perfectly dry, sweat-free face and wondered what he was doing. He walked toward me, took off his backpack, and put it on me!

What was he doing? That thing was heavy. It contained the complete works of Robert Frost. Plus, I was tired and grumpy and sweaty, which made it seem even heavier. Was he nuts? Did he not see me sweating and huffing and puffing? I was about to blow! Watch out, little pigs. In that moment, my super-cute boyfriend did not look super-cute to me. Maybe I had sweat in my eyes. I couldn't see what he was doing. So, I asked him, "Whatever are you doing, darling?" Okay, maybe that's not exactly what I said. It was probably more like, "What the heck do you think you're doing, buddy?" He responded with, "Come here and get on my back. I'll carry you." And instantly, the sweat fell from my eyes and my super-cute boyfriend looked oh-so-handsome once again. And charming. And dashing. He was my hero. And I felt bad for questioning him. He carried me safely up the mountain, on his back, until we reached the very top. And I loved him for it. It is one of my most favorite memories. And it's also one of my most favorite life lessons about God.

There have been many times in my life when I have felt like I was walking up a steep hill. A treacherous mountain. An insurmountable height. And I've struggled. And sweated. And huffed and puffed. I've fallen down. And bruised my knees. And my pride. Sometimes I just quit. I sat down. Refused to move. And in those times, I forgot that God was still with me. Every step of the way. Up the steep mountainside. In the difficult times. He never left my side. In Matthew 11:28–30, Jesus says, "Come to me, all you who are weary and burdened, and I will give you rest. Take my yoke upon you and learn from me, for I am gentle and humble in heart, and you will find rest for your souls. For my yoke is easy and my burden is light."

A yoke is a wooden device, similar to a harness, which fits over the necks of two animals, usually oxen, so they can move together as one. This allows the animals to accomplish their task a little more easily, because they are sharing the load. Jesus asks us to come to him and take his yoke upon our shoulders, so that he can help carry our burdens. There are many times when I feel like I can do things on my own. That I don't need any help. Those are the times when I end up sweaty and out of breath, stranded along the side of a mountain, all alone. But I am not alone. The Lord is always with me. He never leaves my side. He is there, waiting for me to take his yoke upon my shoulders. He will not put it there against my will. He waits for me to come to him. Taking his yoke doesn't mean the burdens disappear, but it does make them easier to carry.

I don't do as much hiking these days, but I still face steep trails and struggles and trials in my life. There will always be mountains to climb. There may not always be a handsome husband to carry me up that hill. But God will always be there, waiting to take my hand and carry me to the top. No sweating required.

PRAYER:

Dear Lord, I know there have been times when you've carried me up that mountain. Thank you for always being by my side. Help me remember that I don't have to walk through this life alone.

TWENTY-TWO

A Jeep was Made for Dirt and Fun

My husband likes trucks. And Jeeps. And machines that are meant to be driven off road through rocky terrain. In his glory days, he drove a Ford F-250 that I affectionately nicknamed "Frankenstein" because it was big and green and didn't have any of its original parts. He loved that truck. It was always dirty. Unfortunately for him, it had to be sold because it just wasn't practical for our growing family. After fifteen years, he still mourns the loss of that vehicle.

A few years ago, he got a crazy idea to buy a Jeep. I'm not talking a new-fangled, fancy Jeep. Nope. I'm talking twenty-five-year-old, dinged-up, rusty beater Jeep. With a manual transmission. A guy he knew was selling one for only twenty-five hundred dollars and apparently this was an absolutely amazing bargain! I did not think this was such a bargain, but what did I know? Apparently, I did not know Jeeps!

My husband's reason for buying this vehicle was to teach our fifteen-year-old daughter how to drive a stick shift. This, he insisted, was a skill that was absolutely necessary for her to learn. And it was non-negotiable. Except in my mind, it wasn't. In my mind, all things were negotiable. Especially the purchase of a twenty-five-year-old rusty hunk of metal.

And so, we negotiated. Well, truthfully, we debated. And argued. Over and over. For the next four months. My position was simple. I did not want to spend twenty-five hundred dollars on a Jeep. I could think of many ways that money could be better spent. Like paying for our daughters' school tuition. Or saving for college. Or paying extra on our mortgage. But spending the money didn't seem to be a problem for him. He thought it was an amazing bargain!

But it wasn't just the purchase price I had an issue with. I honestly didn't care if our daughter learned how to drive a manual transmission. It didn't matter to me one bit. Why couldn't she just learn how to drive in my SUV—which, by the way, was paid for? Okay, I guess it was still a little bit about the money.

My husband said it would be fun! We could take the top off and let the wind blow on our faces. We could go off-roading and not have to worry about getting mud on the tires because that's what a Jeep was made for. Getting mud on the tires. And don't forget about the fun. A Jeep was made for dirt and fun. These may not have been his exact words, but that's how I remember them.

Well, did he think that was going to convince me? Was he new? The dirt and fun did nothing to persuade me. In fact, it kind of did the opposite! All I could imagine was my newly-licensed sixteen-year-old daughter driving eighty-seven miles per hour through the mountains, dirt and gravel flying, getting stuck in the mud and breaking an axle. And being stranded. And alone. In the middle of the mountains. With no cell phone reception. But plenty of dirt! Now I ask you, does this sound like fun? No. No, it does not. Especially not when it gets dark, and she's still stranded and alone in the middle of the mountains. And she's hungry and scared and gets hypothermia from the cold because she had no room for blankets or food in the Jeep because it was too full of fun!

That was what Jeep ownership meant to me. Danger in the

wilderness. Not to mention dangers on the highway. Driving with no doors or roof with the wind whipping her hair. Right into her eyes. And temporarily blinding her so she runs off the road into a ditch. And breaks an axle. And, well, you get the picture.

I did not want to buy that Jeep! I wanted to buy a safe, dependable, non-fun, boring vehicle for our daughter. Maybe a station wagon. Or a minivan. Or a tank. But my husband did not share my sentiments. He felt a Jeep was the best choice. I could not understand this! Why was this so important to him? Why was he so insistent? But he was. And after four months of negotiating, he asked me to trust him. So, I did. And we bought that Jeep.

It turns out that what my husband imagined in buying that Jeep was far different from what I imagined. He imagined time. Buying that Jeep meant time spent with his daughter, teaching her to drive a stick shift. Passing on a skill that he learned at her age. Spending intentional time together. Talking about college and friends and God and the gear shifter. Making time to just be together. To enjoy each other's company. Because he knew that all too soon, the time would slip away. And now was the time to make the most of it together.

And that is why I submitted to my husband's will. Yes, I said submitted. I know submission is a touchy subject. And I admit it has not always been easy for me. But as wives, we are called to submit to our husbands.

Ephesians 5:22–24 says, "Wives, submit yourselves to your own husbands as you do to the Lord. For the husband is the head of the wife as Christ is the head of the church, his body, of which he is the Savior. Now as the church submits to Christ, so also wives should submit to their husbands in everything."

The world tends to view submission in a negative light. It tells us that wives do not have to submit to the authority of their husbands.

In fact, women are often encouraged to assert their authority over men, even their own husbands.

Submission gets a bad rap. It is misunderstood. Submission is simply yielding to the authority of another person. Biblical submission is often misunderstood as well. But it's actually a beautiful thing. As a wife, I submit to my husband when I yield to his leadership, when I choose to follow his authority.

Simply stated, that is submission. Is it always easy? No! Is it always necessary? Yes!

Submission does not mean blindly following everything your husband says and does. It does not mean obeying your husband if it goes against the Word of God. It does not mean doing something illegal or immoral. Submission is not always easy. But when a husband lovingly leads, he makes it easier for his wife to willingly submit.

It took me four months to give in—I mean, submit—to my husband buying that Jeep. But when I took a step back and set my opinions aside, I could see how important it was to him. I could see the value in buying that old Jeep. We weren't investing twenty-five-hundred dollars in a hunk of metal. We were investing that money in our family. My husband knew this from the start. And he was right! I am happy to say that our entire family has enjoyed owning that Jeep! We've had some fun adventures in that hunk of metal.

Just don't ask me to let our daughters go off-roading alone in the mountains. That is non-negotiable!

PRAYER:

Dear Lord, thank you for providing a biblical example of submission in your Word. I want to love my husband in a way that honors you. Help me to have a proper attitude and understanding of submission in my marriage.

TWENTY-THREE

The Gift of Poly-Cotton Blend

Christmas was fast approaching, and I needed to do some shopping for my daughter. She was a senior in high school and would be attending a college in Nashville when she graduated. She was very excited, so I thought she would love to have a sweatshirt that proudly displayed the name of her chosen university. So, one month before Christmas, I began looking for a sweatshirt. Online, of course. We live hundreds of miles from Nashville. The college's online bookstore had quite a few styles to choose from. Some were cute. Others, not so much. I saw a few that I thought my daughter would like, but I wasn't sold on any one in particular. So, I asked my younger daughter for her opinion. She picked one she knew her sister would like. I happened to like it too, so I ordered it. Easy peasy. It would arrive in five to seven business days, in plenty of time for Christmas. Perfect!

The sweatshirt arrived the following week, right on time. Yay! I was excited! And then I wasn't. As I opened the package and pulled out the sweatshirt, I could see it was not the right size. It was clearly too small! I checked the tag. Yep, wrong size. It was a large, and I knew for a fact I had ordered an extra-large. My daughter has a long torso and we often need to order a size up so shirts are long enough to fit her. I checked the packing slip, which stated they had sent me an extra-large, which they clearly had not. They had sent me a large. And it was too short. I admit I was slightly irritated. I believe my reaction was, "Well, I guess Christmas is ruined." I may or may not have overreacted. Just a little. Thankfully, my husband saw my irritation and offered to take care of the situation. He called the bookstore and explained what happened. A sweet lady with a cute Southern accent apologized and said she would send us an extra-large right away. She would also send a prepaid envelope so we could return the large sweatshirt at no cost to us. This was very good news! Christmas was saved!

A few days later, a second package arrived from Nashville. It did, in fact, contain the correct sweatshirt. I should have been happy. But I was not! Although they had sent the sweatshirt in the size I ordered, something didn't look right. This sweatshirt was larger, but it still looked too short. (Long torso, remember?) I tried it on for comparison. It fit fine, until I raised my arms above my head. And then it became a belly shirt. Actually, a belly sweatshirt. Seriously, my entire midriff was showing. Like it was 1982. Only this was not 1982, and I was not Olivia Newton John. I had no desire to "just get physical." I think I heard my body talk. It said, "Take this thing off." My daughter is a good six inches taller than me, with a much longer torso. There was absolutely no way this sweatshirt was going to fit her. Well, wasn't this just lovely! It looked like Christmas was ruined once again.

I was not happy with this turn of events. But I couldn't blame it on the bookstore this time. Nope, this one was on me. I had ordered the extra-large in hopes that it would fit. In my defense, though, I had no idea I was ordering a sweatshirt from the retro department. I now had two sweatshirts, both the wrong size, that needed to be shipped back to Nashville. Good grief! We contacted the bookstore again, and the sweet little Southern lady told us we could stuff both sweatshirts into the return envelope and send them back. Once she received the package, she would refund the money to my account. Yay! One problem solved. Now I needed to order another sweatshirt that would actually fit my daughter. Miss Southern Accent said I could place another order at any time.

So, I did. I decided on a unisex sweatshirt this time, hoping it would be long enough. I placed an order for a large sweatshirt just a few minutes later. Then I drove directly to the nearest UPS drop box and promptly deposited the wrong-sized sweatshirts. Three days later, I received an email stating that my money for the original purchase of the sweatshirts had been refunded. Then three minutes later, I received another email saying I had been refunded the cost of shipping. Soon after, a third email showed the full amount of money that was refunded. The total amount listed in the three emails didn't seem to add up, so I checked my bank balance online. The only problem was that it was Friday evening, after business hours, so the refund had not yet posted. Oh well. I would just have to wait until Monday.

But as I checked my email on Saturday morning, I noticed yet another email from the college bookstore. The very first line caught my attention. It read, "Ya'll, I am so sorry!" Oh no! This could not be good. After reading the message, my feeling was correct. It was not good news. The sweet little Southern bookstore lady explained that when she was cancelling out the original order, she mistakenly cancelled out the new order I had placed for the unisex sweatshirt as well. Oh! My! Goodness! This could not be happening. And now, for the third time in the span of twelve days, Christmas was ruined again! There would be no surprise college sweatshirt waiting to be unwrapped on Christmas morning. There would be no twinkle in my daughter's eye as she opened her gift. Because there would be no sweatshirt. I might as well have taken down the stockings and stuffed the tree "up the chimbly." Why not? I was feeling like the Grinch anyway. Nothing was going according to plan. Things were not working out the way I imagined. That stupid sweatshirt was becoming a thorn in my side.

I couldn't believe this was happening. I confess it took me a few minutes to calm down. Okay, it was more than a few minutes. But once my temper settled, I simply placed yet another order for a large unisex sweatshirt. I double checked the order and quickly hit send, adding a little prayer of "please let it work this time." And then I waited. And three days later, the package arrived, containing the sweatshirt I had ordered. It was perfect! Actually, it looked a little big, but it was close enough. Christmas was saved! Finally! As my daughter opened her presents on Christmas morning, she smiled, happy to receive the gift. She had no idea the ordeal I had gone through to get her that sweatshirt. So, I told her the entire story. And we all laughed.

But when I was in the midst of the chaos, I was not laughing. Why had I been so irritated? Why had I declared—more than once—that Christmas was ruined? Because of misplaced hope. I had placed my hope for a glorious Christmas in a poly-cotton blend sweatshirt. What was I thinking? I had a picture in my mind of how I wanted Christmas to look. I wanted snow on the ground with a cozy fire roaring in the fireplace while we sat around the tree and sipped hot cocoa, basking in the warmth of our love for one another. I wanted to live out the "picture print by Currier and Ives." Realistically, I knew this was impossible. But it didn't keep me from hoping.

The problem was, I had placed my hope in the wrong thing. I should have placed my hope in Jesus. I should have focused on his miraculous birth. But I let myself get distracted. I got caught up in trying to manufacture my very own perfect Christmas. What I really did was set myself up for disappointment. Scripture says, "May the God of hope fill you with all joy and peace as you trust in him, so that you may overflow with hope by the power of the Holy Spirit" (Romans 15:13). When I refocused my hope on God, I wasn't disappointed at all.

There was no snow on the ground Christmas morning, my youngest daughter had a cold, and I don't remember anyone sipping hot chocolate. But we still had a lovely Christmas. Because our hope was placed in the birth of Jesus.

Next Christmas, I will try to remember that true hope can only be found in swaddling clothes, not in a poly-cotton blend.

PRAYER:

Lord, you are the true and living hope. Thank you
for sending your love in the form of a baby. Help
me to keep my eyes fixed on the true meaning of
Christmas, the gift of salvation through your Son.

TWENTY-FOUR

Beware of Fast-Moving Minivans

My husband and I like to go for walks. Taking a walk in the evening helps us connect. We talk about our day, the kids, or whatever else comes to mind. Plus, there's the added benefit of fresh air and exercise! We live on a rural road, so there is no shoulder to speak of. But there are trees and hills and apple orchards. The road is winding and steep in spots, so we try to stay off to the side as much as we can to avoid coming into direct contact with cars. Some days we don't see any cars at all, but other days we see quite a few. Cars on our road tend to drive very fast! Which is why we do our walking in the daylight, mostly.

One evening after dinner, my husband asked if I'd like to go for a walk. Now, ordinarily I would jump at the chance to go walking with my handsome husband. But it was already beginning to get dark. Almost dusky. And I do not like to walk up our road in the darkness. Or even near-darkness. So, I voiced my concern. I said, "Yes, I'd love to go for a walk. But it's getting dark. It might not be safe." He said that I had nothing to fear because he would protect me. My husband is wonderful. He's tall and strong and rugged. But he is not Superman. How did he think he was going to protect me from a speeding truck or distracted minivan? So I asked him, "How are you going to protect me from a two-ton, fast-moving vehicle?" His response? "I will push you down a hill."

Oh, he's a charmer, that one. Did I mention his dry sense of humor? And yet I still love him! I momentarily glared at him. And then he smiled at me in his annoyingly charming, yet incredibly handsome way and said, "I'd do it too, you know. I'd push you down that hill. If a car was flying toward us, out of control, I'd push you down the hill to save you. Because I love you." And I had no doubt he would do it. He would push me down that hill. To save me. Because he loves me.

But as much as my husband loves me, God loves me even more. And although my husband is big and strong and an amazing protector, God is even bigger and stronger. He shields me. He protects me. He keeps me from harm. He goes before me and behind me.

Isaiah 52:12 says, "But you will not leave in haste or go in flight; for the LORD will go before you, the God of Israel will be your rear guard." Simply put, a rear guard is a soldier who is positioned at the rear of the troops in order to protect from any attack that may come from behind. (I didn't know this. I had to look it up!)

God has me covered on all sides! He goes before me to clear a path for me to follow him. He walks into the battle ahead of me and shields me from the enemy. But he also brings up the rear. He guards me from dangers that may come from behind. Things I may not see. Like an arrow from the enemy. Or a fast-moving Subaru! And that's why I welcome a shove down the hill. I know that what is best for me isn't always pleasant. But it is always necessary.

So, I thank the Lord for his protection, from all sides. And, I thank my husband for protecting me, too. For being an example of God's love for me. And yes, I even thank him for his willingness to push me down a hill. Because that, my friends, is true love!

PRAYER:

Lord, thank you for your watchful care over me.
You are my shield and fortress. I trust you to
protect me in all of life's circumstances.

TWENTY-FIVE

Magnets Are Not a Tasty Snack

When my daughter was three years old, she swallowed a poop pellet. Yep, you read that right. A poop pellet! It was from a Barbie doll toy set that came with a dog and little round brown magnetic pellets, about the size of a pea. When you put a pellet in the dog's mouth, the dog would "eat" it and then "poop" it out when you pulled his tail. Wow! Sounds weird, I know. And gross! I mean, if you think about it, the dog was essentially eating his own poop! Who thinks of these things, anyway? But my daughter loved it! Apparently three-year-olds think magnetic poop pellets are great fun. So, I guess that makes the toy company genius. Because they obviously got us to buy one for our daughter.

One day, my sweet little girl was playing with the Barbies. She liked to play with all the Barbies and all the accessories at the same time. She would dump the Barbie bin into a heap on the floor and sort through all the shoes and purses and clothes until she found what she was looking for. And I would play with her. That's what happens when you only have two kids. You become the designated playmate for one child when the other child is at school. I loved playing with my girls. Really, I did. But after one hour and forty-two minutes of dressing the same two Barbies in the same two outfits (or several variations of the same), you tend to get distracted. Okay, bored. Let's just be honest here. First I became bored, and then I got distracted. And that is apparently when my sweet little three-year-old decided it would be fun to eat fake Barbie dog poop.

She walked right up to me and said, "Mama, I ate the poop." Now, under normal circumstances, I would have been completely freaked out. But given the fact that she was holding a toy dog in one hand and a pile of poop pellets in the other, I was fairly confident she had not eaten the real thing. But I still panicked. A little. I mean, ingesting a magnet, no matter how small, was probably not good for her digestive system.

So, I called the doctor, and oh what a fun conversation that was! I had to explain to a well-educated pediatrician that my daughter had swallowed a poop pellet. The conversation went something like this: "She was playing with Barbies and she put a dog poop pellet in her mouth. I didn't actually see it happen but she said she swallowed it. It's magnetic. And round. And very small. About the size of a pea. A small, round, pea-sized, magnetic poop pellet. Will she be okay? What should I do?" And after the doctor finished laughing (no joke, she laughed), she told me that because it was so small and smooth, with no rough edges, it should pass through her digestive system within three to five days with no problem. But I would have to check to make sure it had exited her system.

Umm, what? I would have to check? Sure! No problem! That sounded easy enough. How hard could it be to find a tiny brown pea-sized poop pellet in normal everyday brown poop? There was no way I would be able to spot it just by observation. No, this job called for a hands-on approach.

For the next three days, I literally had to squish her poop. Each time my daughter went to the bathroom, I went along with her. I perched on the edge of the tub, wearing disposable latex gloves, and waited. If she produced a #2, I picked it up and squished, feeling for something hard, in search of that elusive poop pellet. This was not a fun time. I repeated the process for three days in a row until I finally felt something hard. Sure enough, she had finally pooped out the poop pellet! Hooray! We both squealed in delight. And then my sweet little three-year-old looked at me with her beautiful brown eyes and asked, "Can I keep it?" Seriously. No joke. She wanted to keep the pea-sized poop pellet.

I said no, of course. I told her it was yucky and it wouldn't work anymore and now it was just like real poop so we had to flush it down the toilet with the other poop. And she believed me! So, flush it we did!

I didn't think of this at the time because I was just so happy I no longer had to squish the poop, but isn't this situation just like real life? Now hopefully we don't go around swallowing poop pellets, but what about sin? How much sin and junk and badness do we allow in our lives? We welcome it in. Swallow it down without hesitation. We let it live inside us. It works its way into the very depths of our soul and settles in to stay. We know it's not good for us. We know it shouldn't be there. And deep down we want to be rid of it. So, we ask for God's help and forgiveness. And he forgives. Because he loves us. But sometimes, once we are rid of the sin, instead of being happy to let it go, we want it back! We become so attached to our sin, we don't know if we can function without it. Like my daughter wanting to keep the poop pellet, we want to hold on to the very thing that isn't good for us. That little round magnetic pellet literally came out in her poop and she wanted to keep it! Now, she was only three years old and didn't know any better. But we should know better!

Scripture says, "Forget the former things; do not dwell on the past" (Isaiah 43:18). In other words, leave the mess behind. God has better things in store for you! Verse 19 goes on to say, "See, I am doing a new thing! Now it springs up; do you not perceive it? I am making a way in the desert and streams in the wasteland." God will make a way for you. But you have to leave the past behind. You cannot move forward until you get rid of the junk he has already freed you from.

Getting rid of the junk can be messy work. Trust me, I know. But that magnetic poop pellet did not belong in my daughter. And sin does not belong in you. What do you need to get rid of today? Time to flush away that junk! No squishing required.

PRAYER:

Lord, you are amazing! Thank you for working in my life, behind the scenes, making a way for me. I know my life is full of yucky things. Help me to let go, flush them away, and make room for the good works you want to do in my life.

TWENTY-SIX

Never Trust a Car Named Bob

We recently bought an SUV. His name is Bob. Actually, his full name is Bob Ross. This is what my daughter named him, for some reason. And, for some reason, the name just stuck.

I like Bob Ross. He is a good, reliable, comfortable vehicle with good gas mileage. He is painted a very fetching shade of green. At four years old, he is the newest vehicle we've ever owned. But he is new to me, and I don't know him very well yet. I tend to be slow in trusting new people, including cars—and Bob Ross is no exception. He has not yet gained my trust. Let me tell you why.

One hot summer afternoon, we decided to take a drive to visit family. My husband and I, along with our two daughters, climbed into Bob Ross and started out on an hour-long journey. I noticed that we were running low on gas. And I do not like to run much below a quarter of a tank. So of course, I suggested that we stop to fill Bob up before we hit the highway. I thought this was a sensible suggestion. My husband? Not so much! You see, he's more of a "let's see how far we can run on fumes" kind of guy. He suggested that we not stop to get gas. Bob Ross came equipped with a fancy digital gauge that displayed the number of miles that could be traveled on a tank of gas. The gauge was reading sixty miles, which, according to my husband, meant we could travel another sixty miles before the tank would be empty. I, however, did not yet trust Bob Ross. I had only known him a few short weeks. We were practically strangers!

I really wanted to stop for gas, despite my husband's faith in our new vehicle. But before I could say another word, Bob Ross did a strange thing. His digital gauge suddenly turned from sixty to fifty! Yep, he dropped ten miles! And I knew for a fact that we had only driven five miles. Nope, Bob Ross could not be trusted. That was it! Surely my husband could see we needed to stop for gas. But he did not agree! He wanted to put Bob Ross to the test. Could we really go another fifty miles? Or maybe more than fifty miles? He was convinced we could make it to our destination without stopping to refuel. My husband is the trusting kind. So, he kept on driving. Right by the only gas station we would pass before we reached the highway. At this point, I had a choice to make. I could keep quiet and silently support my husband's attempt to make it to our destination without stopping for fuel. Or I could voice my opinion and strongly—yet sweetly—suggest once again that we stop for gas, for goodness' sake! By now you might not be surprised to learn that I chose the latter.

Before I could point out that Bob could not be trusted, the fancy digital gas gauge once again dropped ten miles. Yep, that's right. From fifty to forty! In just over two miles. Bob was obviously not honest. He was, in fact, a liar. Or at the very least, a fibber. We needed to stop for gas. ASAP! But as we drove onto the interstate, I realized Bob was in cahoots with my husband. They must have worked out a plan when I wasn't looking. A plan to test my patience. Or to make me crazy. Or maybe have some sort of heart episode. At this point I'd had enough. My mouth took over! I not-so-calmly asked my husband if he had seen the latest reading on the gas gauge. I asked if he was trying to drive me crazy. I asked if he had any regard for the fact that I was about to have a full-blown panic attack! He gave me one of his mischievous smiles. Yes, he had seen the gas gauge. No, he was not going to stop. Apparently, Bob Ross was his new best friend. Apparently, he trusted Bob Ross more than he trusted his very own oh-so-smart and loving wife of twenty-two years! Apparently, he had forgotten that I was almost always right.

So, I zipped my lips, crossed my arms, and threw an "oh, you better know what you're doing, buddy" look in my husband's direction. And then I waited. In silence. As we sped down the highway. I must admit that the next ten miles were uneventful. Bob's gauge seemed stuck at forty. It hadn't moved at all. Which was suspicious! And trust me, I was keeping my eyeball glued to that fancy gauge! As each mile passed and we came closer to our destination, my husband's confidence in Bob grew. Mine, however, did not. We did manage to make it another eight miles before Bob's gauge dropped to thirty. Okay, eight miles was close to ten miles. I would let it slide. This time. At this point, we were only ten miles from our destination. And Bob was now saying we could make it another thirty miles. Even if he was off by ten miles, we just might be able to make it. My confidence grew by a tiny ounce.

And then it deflated completely!

Just as the gauge hit thirty miles, Bob made a strange sound. And then he bucked. Seriously, bucked! Like a bronco at the rodeo. And then Bob slowed down. On the interstate! With cars zipping past us going 75 mph! I gasped. And clutched my chest. What was happening? Had we run over something? Did Bob blow a tire? And then I knew. We! Had! Run! Out! Of! Gas! On the highway!

Panic ensued. I don't recall my exact words, but I'm sure I yelled something not so pleasant at my husband. And I may or may not have shouted, "I told you so!" Thankfully, my husband is a quick thinker, and he does not panic easily. He steered Bob off the highway and onto the nearest off-ramp. We made it halfway up the ramp, and then Bob died. Right there on a turn. With cars flying past us. In the hot summer sun. On the off-ramp!

Well, wasn't this a lovely turn of events? Now what? After boring a hole in my husband's soul with my angry laser eyes, we carefully exited the vehicle. Because Bob was too hot. Because he had died. Therefore, there was no air conditioning. So, we stood on the side of the road, in the weeds, with cars flying past, on the turn of the exit ramp. I called my sister. I explained our plight. I asked her for help. She laughed and said she would send my nephew over right away with a gas can. And so, we waited. In the scorching summer sun. In the weeds. On the side of the off-ramp.

Three cars stopped to ask if we needed help, bless their hearts. We thanked them and assured them help would be arriving soon. My nephew, the hero, showed up in under ten minutes, gas can in hand, and filled our tank with enough fuel to get us safely to the nearest gas station. God bless him.

My husband apologized profusely. He said he should have trusted me. He said he should have gotten gas before we hit the highway. And then he said, "You're going to write about this, aren't you?" Oh yes, my friend! I am so going to write about this! Because there is a lesson to be learned here. And not just the obvious "you should always listen to your wife" lesson. But a lesson about trust. Or rather, misplaced trust.

Scripture is full of warnings about trust. Psalm 146:3 says, "Do not put your trust in princes, in human beings, who cannot save." And Psalm 118:8–9 says, "It is better to take refuge in the LORD than to trust in humans. It is better to take refuge in the LORD than to trust in princes." And my personal favorite, Jeremiah 17:5–6: "This is what the LORD says: 'Cursed is the one who trusts in man, who draws strength from mere flesh and whose heart turns away from the LORD. That person will be like a bush in the wastelands; they will not see prosperity when it comes. They will dwell in the parched places of the desert, in a salt land where no one lives.'"

Well, isn't that just exactly like what happened to us! We (well, not me, my husband. Sorry honey!) put our trust in a vehicle. Okay, so not an actual person but his name is Bob Ross so it's kind of like a person. His trust was misplaced! He should not have trusted Bob. In fact, Jeremiah 17:5 actually says the one who puts his trust in man is cursed! Ouch! Our trust should only be placed in the Lord. Not in a person, or a vehicle with a fancy digital gas gauge. Verse six goes on to say that if you put your trust in man, you will dwell in parched places of the desert. Now I know the side of the highway on a hot summer afternoon is not actually the Mojave Desert. But let me tell you, it was plenty hot! Too hot for me. I would never want to dwell in the parched desert—literally or figuratively.

The good news is that Scripture offers hope. "But blessed is the one who trusts in the LORD, whose confidence is in him. They will be like a tree planted by the water that sends out its roots by the stream. It does not fear when heat comes; its leaves are always green. It has no worries in a year of drought and never fails to bear fruit" (Jeremiah 17:7–8).

I sure could have used a cool stream while I was standing in the weeds along the off-ramp in the blazing hot summer sun. I do not like the blistering heat. I much prefer to be cool. And also, not stranded. The truth is, when I put my trust in the Lord, I do not have to fear the heat! When my confidence is in God, life is a little less scary. I can always trust that he will lead me and protect me and guide me safely off the interstate. He will never leave me stranded. When I put my trust in man (or a green SUV named Bob), I will be disappointed. Because trust in man is a false trust.

A false hope. A false sense of security. Trust in God is true. I don't need to worry when I put my trust in him, because God himself is truth. God will never lie. God will never give me a false reading on a fancy digital gas gauge.

And if I put me trust in him, he will never leave me stranded on the side of the highway.

PRAYER:

Lord, you are faithful and trustworthy. Thank you for
your promise that if I put my trust in you, I do not
have to fear. May I always place my trust in you!

TWENTY-SEVEN

Ducks Can't Swim on a Frozen Pond

My grandparents lived in a beautiful setting way out in the country. When I was a child, I loved going to their house to visit. It seemed like such a magical place. I loved swinging on the porch swing, playing in the yard, and taking walks with my grandfather, affectionately known as Pappap!

Just down the road from their house was a little duck pond. Every time we visited, Pap would take my sisters and me to the pond to feed the ducks. We loved going to that pond! One Christmas when I was a teenager, Pap and I decided to take a walk to the pond. It was very cold, and we knew the ducks wouldn't be there because they had already flown south to warmer weather. But we took a walk to the pond anyway, just me and Pap.

As we came closer to the pond, we could see that it was mostly frozen, but there was still water around the edges, along with some very thin patches of ice. We began chatting about Christmas and the weather and ducks, when out of the blue, Pap said, "I wonder if the pond is frozen the whole way through?" I replied that it probably was not frozen the whole way through, because you could see water around the edges of the ice.

What Pap did next nearly gave me a heart attack, or a panic attack, or some kind of "good grief, you scared me half to death" attack! He stepped onto the pond! Yep, my seventy-something-year-old grandfather, wearing his heavy shoes, winter coat, and adorable corduroy hat with insulated ear flaps took a step onto that ice. And then he took another step! I was momentarily rendered speechless. It must have been shock or something, or maybe my lips were frozen from the cold because I couldn't seem to move them. My brain was screaming, "No! Don't do it! Get off the ice!" But my mouth just wouldn't cooperate.

As soon as my lips thawed, I yelled, "Pap! Get off the ice! What in the world are you doing? Are you nuts?" But Pap did not reply. He just kept walking. Well, it was really more like a shuffle. Like he was ice skating, except he wasn't wearing skates! Right foot forward, then the left, and then the right again.

All I could do was watch. And yell. Unwillingly, my brain started playing awful scenarios in my mind. I imagined that any second the ice would crack and my beloved grandfather would swiftly fall into the depths of the frigid December pond, leaving only his cute little corduroy hat behind, floating on an iceberg. And I would run back to the house, the bearer of bad news, soggy hat in hand, and ruin Christmas day for my family for all eternity! What an imagination!

I kept my eyes on Pap the entire time he was on the pond. I could not peel them away. I kept yelling, pleading, begging him to turn around and get off that ice. But he kept on going, shuffling his way right toward the center of the pond.

My attempts to coax him off the pond had thus far been in vain, but I had to give it one more try. I called out to him, "Pap, please turn around! Get off the ice! If you fall in, I won't be able to save you. I can't swim!" He stopped in his tracks, looked over his shoulder and said, "That's alright, I can't swim either!" And with a sassy smile and a mischievous laugh, he continued his trek across the semi-frozen pond until he finally reached the other side. It was the longest two minutes of my life!

To be clear, I would never suggest stepping onto a semi-frozen pond just to test the water. But what my grandfather did on that long-ago December day was a perfect example of faith, and placing your trust in God. Stepping out into the unknown, unafraid of what might happen, because you know the Lord is in control.

Joshua chapter three tells the story of how the Levites crossed the Jordan River while carrying the Ark of the Covenant. Joshua and the Israelites were camped by the Jordan. After three days, they were instructed to follow the Ark of the Covenant when they saw it passing by. The Lord instructed Joshua to have the priests take up the Ark and carry it to the edge of the Jordan's waters and then go stand in the river (v. 8). Now this might not seem like a big deal, until you read verse fifteen. It says the Jordan River was at flood stage, which means the level of the water had risen above the banks, spilling over onto the shores.

I myself am not a fan of water. Especially when I can't see the bottom. I don't like to step into anything when I can't see where my feet will land. But that is what the Lord instructed the priests to do! And they did it! We read in Joshua chapter three that "as soon as the priests who carried the ark reached the Jordan and their feet touched the water's edge, the water from upstream stopped flowing. It piled up in a heap a great distance away . . . So the people crossed over opposite Jericho. The priests who carried the ark of the covenant of the LORD stopped in the middle of the Jordan and stood on dry ground, while all Israel passed by until the whole nation had completed the crossing on dry ground" (vv. 15–17).

That is truly amazing! That is blind faith! Those priests had no way of knowing what would happen when they stepped into the roaring waters of the Jordan River. They did not ask questions. They did not turn and run away.

Honestly, if it were me, I don't think I would have been as eager to step into that river. And I know I would not have been silent. I would have panicked and asked 10,000 questions. Like, "Why are we doing this?" Or "Hey Joshua, are you sure you heard exactly what the Lord said? I know you're just getting over that cold. Maybe your ears are still clogged." Or what about "Why don't we build a raft and float across? Seems like a sensible solution to me!"

But the Levites did not question God. They hoisted up the Ark and marched directly to the river. And even when they saw the banks of the swollen river, they did not stop. They plunged straight into that raging water, sandals and all! They could have stopped and waited and asked the Lord to calm the raging river, or build a bridge, or part the waters. (Where's Moses when you need him?) But they didn't stop. And that is where their faith came into action! They stepped into the water, without stopping, without question, without hesitation, and without life vests! And only after stepping into the river did the Lord calm the water, stop it from flowing, and heap it up downstream.

That, my friends, is a true picture of faith!

How does this apply to my life? Faith! Trusting in the Lord. Believing that what he says is true. Knowing that he knows the future, even when we can't possibly know it. Stepping out in faith and stepping into the chaos and craziness and seemingly impossible. But with God all things are possible (Matthew 19:26).

Are you ready to take a step of faith? To put on your sandals and go wading in that river? Go lace up your boots and step onto that ice. Figuratively, of course. I would not suggest walking on a semi-frozen pond!

PRAYER:

Thank you, Lord, for being faithful and trustworthy. I want to follow where you lead me, even if it seems scary. Please help me to take that step of faith.

TWENTY-EIGHT

A Church Rock Star Wears Khaki Pants

My husband is a social butterfly. That doesn't sound very manly, does it? Where does that term come from, anyway? There should really be another phrase for "socially adept, friendly extrovert who enjoys talking to people, even strangers!" How about social lion? No, that sounds too intimidating. How about social buck (you know, like a deer). That sounds manly. But, no. Too ego-inducing. What about social husky puppy? That sounds sweet and manly all at the same time. But somehow, I don't think that fits, either.

But, whatever! My husband is a friendly, fun-loving, social kind of guy. Me? Not so much. I am more of an introvert. Now don't get me wrong. I'm nice and friendly and I'll smile and say hello, but I do not usually seek out a conversation or attention. Of any kind. Especially from strangers! And there's a fifty-fifty chance that even if I know you, I still may not talk to you. I'll just smile and wave from a distance. It's not that I don't like people at all. I do like people. Well, some people. It's just that people are so people-y! And crowds of people are a definite no-no. I would much rather sit on my couch, under a blanket, coffee cup in hand, and read a good book. Or watch reruns of The Andy Griffith Show. Seriously my favorite TV show of all time!

Oh, I have friends. And I like to talk to my friends. But I'm not so good with new people. Or even large groups of people that I already know. I can handle a handful of people. But once I get past a handful or two, I tend to shut down. Or fade into the background. And that's where my husband and I differ. He doesn't mind people. In fact, I think he actually likes them. He interacts with people all day long. It's his job. He meets with clients, some of whom he's never met before!

He's also great in social situations. If we go to a party, even at a friend's house, I scope out a chair in the corner of the room and plant myself there for the remainder of the evening. But not my husband. He flits around talking first to one person and then another. Like a butterfly flitting from flower to flower. Oh! And there it is! Social butterfly! Mystery solved.

And you should see him at church! He's like a rock star. Yep, a rock star in khaki pants and dress shoes. Seriously, he's like church royalty or something. As soon as we walk in the door, someone calls out his name from across the foyer. Or fist bumps him. Then his buddies all line up and do the wave in honor of his arrival. Okay, this is a slight exaggeration, but certainly not completely impossible. We can barely take five steps down the hall before someone stops to talk to him. Not me. Him.

Oh, I get the standard, "Good morning. How are you?" And I give the standard, "Fine. How are you?" But that's usually the extent of it. Three seconds after walking into church, my rock star is in deep conversation with one of his buddies. Talking about football or hunting. Or making plans to go hunting. Or going to the all-you-can-eat oyster feed at the fire hall. Meanwhile, I stand beside him, smiling like an idiot, trying to nudge him down the hall so we are not late to Sunday school—again. I do not like to be late, because then everyone stares at me as I enter the room. And I do not like to be in the spotlight. No thank you!

So, I have learned to be comfortably uncomfortable. What does this mean, you ask? It means that I do not have to feel comfortable in the same situations that my husband feels comfortable in. I do not have to serve in the same way he serves. I never know what he is going to be asked to do on any given Sunday morning. He could easily be asked to help move tables or stack chairs or fill in for a sick usher. And his answer is always yes. Because he is kind and considerate and he enjoys serving in these ways.

I've learned that I do not like to be the center of attention. I prefer to cheer people on from the sidelines. I would rather work behind the scenes. I will make you muffins when you are sick. I will send you a cheerful note when you're having a bad day. I will clean your house for you after you've had surgery. But I will not volunteer to teach your Bible study. I will not organize the canned food drive. I will not be the "toilet paper bride" at your sister's bridal shower. And I will by no means be in the Christmas pageant dressed as a shepherd.

But my husband will. Except for that toilet paper bride thing. And that is okay! Because he is the social butterfly that he is. And I am the hibernating bear that I am. But we both have something to offer. It's just not the same something!

In 1 Corinthians 12:4–6, Paul says, "There are different kinds of gifts, but the same Spirit distributes them. There are different kinds of service, but the same Lord. There are different kinds of working, but in all of them and in everyone it is the same God at work." Did you catch that? The key word is different. Different kinds of gifts. Different kinds of service. But the same God! We are all different. God gives us all different giftings, abilities, and personalities. And tolerance levels for large groups of people. We do not all have to be the church rock star in khaki pants. Or the blueberry muffin maker. But we should all use the gifts God has given us to serve him, and to serve others.

Scripture reminds us that "each of you should use whatever gift you have received to serve others, as faithful stewards of God's grace in its various forms" (1 Peter 4:10). Of course, this applies to singing and teaching and serving and preaching. But it also applies to table moving and muffin making.

So, I will be happy to make you fresh blueberry muffins. Or banana nut. Or peanut butter chocolate chip. And my husband will deliver them with a smile, a friendly handshake (or fist bump), and probably an offer to mow your lawn. And if you need me, I'll be the one waving from the car!

PRAYER:

Lord, you are loving and generous. Thank you for giving
me my own unique gifts. Please help me use them
to encourage others and show them your love.

TWENTY-NINE

Put On Your Armor and Climb into the Passenger's Seat

Driving with a teenager is fun. And by fun, I mean nerve-wracking. And scary. And sweat-inducing. Now let me be clear. My teenager is a good driver. Now. But not at first. I mean really, no one is a good driver at first. It takes practice. And time. And learning. Just like a baby. A baby can't walk when she is first born. Well, at least not a human baby. I think cows can walk when they're born. And giraffes. But not humans. It takes months before a baby discovers what her legs are for. It takes lots of practice and falling down and bruised knees before a baby can walk on her own. And so it is with driving. It takes practice. Lots and lots and lots of practice. Long hours of driving with a sixteen-year-old behind the wheel of a two-ton motorized vehicle. And an oh-so-lucky parent (that's me) sitting in the passenger's seat with sweaty hands and knees knocking out a steady rhythm.

Again, I want to say that my daughter is a good driver. Very responsible. But somehow that does nothing to lessen my anxiety. Not at first, anyway. Climbing into the passenger's seat for the first time with a teenage driver is like climbing into the seat of a roller coaster when you're afraid of heights. Or don't like roller coasters. (That's me! I don't like roller coasters.) But nonetheless, you climb in that seat just the same. You fasten your seat belt, grab onto the "Jesus help me" bar, say a quick prayer, and take a shot of whiskey. Just kidding. But you do get in the car with your kid, out of extreme love for her. I mean, why else would you put yourself in this situation? You wouldn't! The answer is you wouldn't.

Your baby wants to learn to drive. Just like all the other babies, I mean teens. And it is your job as a responsible parent to teach your baby how to drive. How to navigate the road. How to watch out for danger. How to safely drive in the rain and snow. How to change lanes and use the windshield wipers. How to drive on the highway and parallel park. Actually, this is not my job. It's her father's job!

I want my daughter to learn these things. I want her to gain all the skills necessary for safely operating a motor vehicle, while never driving over 35 mph. Because driving a car is a big responsibility. I'm talking huge. Like "Stay Puft Marshmallow Man" sized! Sometimes, in my enthusiasm as an expert driving instructor, I offer helpful suggestions. And by helpful suggestions I mean direct orders. Typically spoken in a moment of distress or panic or a sense of impending doom. Orders like, "Hit the brakes!" Or "Watch out for that car!" Of course, I do actually offer helpful suggestions as well. Like, "The light is red." Or "Turn your wipers on. It's raining." You know, obvious suggestions that may not always be obvious. But I feel the need to impart my wisdom to my teenage driver. Sometimes she heeds my warnings, I mean instructions. And sometimes she does not. But I think it's because she just doesn't hear me. Maybe she suffers from temporary deafness. It's obviously not her fault.

There are just so many things she needs to learn! Of course, she must learn the rules of the road and all that safety stuff. But she also needs to know how to properly adjust the seat after father has been driving the car. I want her to know the importance of programming the best radio stations. And the volume. Finding the perfect volume for her listening comfort. After all, one day she will be driving on her own. Alone. Without me in the passenger seat to guide her. (Oh, my goodness. I seriously just had chest pain!) But that is the goal. Not my chest pain. Independence for her. From me. From her father. (Gulp! There's that pain again. Can someone please remove this anvil from my chest?)

But we hope and pray she never achieves independence from God. He is an expert driving instructor. Our ultimate goal in life should be dependence upon God, not independence from him. Scripture says, "Trust in the LORD with all your heart and lean not on your own understanding; in all your ways submit to him, and he will make your paths straight" (Proverbs 3:5–6). How's that for driving instruction? Keeping God in the passenger's seat guarantees straight roads. Figuratively, of course. But words to live by just the same.

Much like a devoted parent teaching her sixteen-year-old the rules of the road, God instructs us because he loves us. He guides us around those menacing curves. He maneuvers us around potholes. He alerts us to unforeseen dangers. And sometimes he takes us on detours. All while giving expert instruction. But first, we have to open the door and let him in the vehicle. And then we have to listen to his voice. We have to acknowledge him and heed his instruction. We cannot shut him out or claim temporary deafness like a teenager with an attitude. Because driving through life without God is scarier than driving with an inexperienced sixteen-year-old. Or a slightly sweaty, nervous, knee-knocking mother. (Just ask my daughter.) So, what are you waiting for? Invite God into your two-ton motorized vehicle, otherwise known as life. He will never steer you wrong!

PRAYER:

Dear Lord, thank you for guiding me on the road of
life. Help me to always heed your instruction and
stay on the path you have laid out for me.

THIRTY

Beware of Falling Mustache Hairs

My husband has a beautiful beard. And when I say beautiful, I, of course, mean rugged and manly and oh-so-handsome. It's true! I love his beard. It is soft and full and tinged with gray, which I think makes him look all the more attractive.

He's had a beard literally all the years I've known him. In all that time, he's only shaved it off once. And that was only because his mother requested that he remove it for his senior pictures. Which he did, against his will. It was not a good look for him!

And there was one time when he went to a new barber and he came home looking like he had the mange. Seriously. His beard was thin in some spots and patchy in others. He looked like he had leprosy. I should have dunked him in the bathtub seven times. Somehow, I don't think that would have worked out well for either of us.

But other than those two instances, I have always loved his beard. Of course, he has a mustache too, and not just a beard. He's not Amish. I like the look of the mustache in conjunction with the beard. It all blends well together. But I am not, I repeat, NOT a fan of a lone mustache. Oh no! A mustache without a beard is just sad face fuzz that draws unnecessary attention to your nose and upper lip.

I do not like the look of a solo mustache. Unless, of course, that mustache is on the face of Tom Selleck. In my humble opinion, Tom Selleck is the only man on the face of the earth who looks good with a solitary mustache. Of course, he looks good without a mustache, too. But that is totally not the point.

Back to my husband's furry face. He keeps his beard and mustache well groomed, which he does mostly for me. If it were solely up to him, he would grow his facial hair out until he looked like Jeremiah Johnson. Or Sasquatch. But he loves me too much to do that. Oh, I don't mind his beard being longer and fuller. I just like it to be nicely shaped. I'm not a fan of those wily hairs that stick out in all directions and refuse to be tamed by a comb and beard oil.

And oh, that mustache! Have you ever heard a mustache referred to as a soup strainer? Umm . . . eww! If the hair grows too far over the top lip, it does, in fact, become a strainer of sorts. A milk strainer. A scrapple trapper. A late-night-pepper-jelly-cracker-snack-oh-please-wipe-that-thing-before-you-kiss-me catcher!

So yes, he keeps his fur well-groomed. Mostly. For which I am very thankful. He goes to the barber usually every four weeks or so, but sometimes he stretches it out a few weeks longer. And he doesn't like for his mustache to grow too long, either. So, he often trims it himself. He used to let me trim it. Okay, once. He let me trim it once. Early on, when we hadn't been married very long. But for some reason, I started laughing and I couldn't stop. So my hand began shaking and those sharp little scissors poked him right in the lip. And for some reason that made me laugh even harder. Until he snatched the scissors out of my hand and quickly ran to the mirror to inspect his slightly bloody lip. He has never let me trim his mustache again!

One night, the old scrapple-trapper was getting a little too long, and my husband decided it was time for a trim. So, before he came to bed, he pulled out his trimmers and got to work. I could hear the buzz of those electric clippers (he doesn't trust scissors anymore). Then I heard him rinsing the hairs down the drain. It was dark when he came to bed, so I couldn't see his face, but I knew when he kissed me there would be no chance of coming into contact with any leftovers from dinner!

As he climbed into bed, I turned toward him, anticipating my goodnight kiss. And that's when it happened. As he leaned in to kiss me, a stray mustache hair fell directly into my mouth! I gagged. And coughed. I tried to spit it out. I sat straight up and cracked my head. Right into his head. He asked me what was wrong. I couldn't speak. I was choking. I needed a drink of water! I forced myself to breathe slowly. Once I calmed down long enough to catch my breath, I said in a rather hoarse voice, "You dropped a mustache hair into my mouth!" He immediately apologized and then started laughing. And once I realized I wasn't going to choke to death, I started laughing, too.

You know, that stray little mustache hair is kind of like the devil. Yep, I said it. Like the devil! There I was, innocently minding my own business, looking forward to a goodnight kiss from my hubby, when out of nowhere that pesky hair jumped right into my mouth. Uninvited. Unbidden. And most certainly unwelcome! And that is how the devil works!

Scripture reminds us to "be alert and of sober mind. Your enemy the devil prowls around like a roaring lion looking for someone to devour" (1 Peter 5:8). Satan is sneaky. He's tricky. He prowls around looking for someone to devour, and then he attacks!

The thing is, I had no idea I would be accosted by a wily mustache hair. I was only expecting a kiss from my husband. I didn't know a stray hair was lurking under his nose just waiting to be let loose. I wasn't standing guard against mustache hairs! After all, I had heard the hairs being rinsed down the sink. I thought I was safe. I let my guard down. Actually, I didn't even know I had to be on guard against facial hair!

And just like that little stray mustache hair, the devil lies in wait for us to drop our guard. He looks for our weakness and vulnerability. And then without warning, he pounces! Like a lion, he attacks when we are at our lowest and most vulnerable. And that is why the Scripture says to be alert. To be vigilant. Quick to take notice of dangerous circumstances. We must always be on guard against the devil's schemes.

And how do we do that? By walking with the Lord and being in his Word daily. When you walk in step with the Lord, you are far more likely to see impending danger and have time to get out of the way!

So, the next time my husband trims his mustache, I will kindly ask him to sweep his face before kissing me. But just to be safe, I'll be on full alert!

PRAYER:

Dear Lord, that devil sure is a sneaky one! But I know you are greater and stronger! I want to walk in step with you. Open my eyes to any impending danger in my path today.

THIRTY-ONE

Don't Sniff the Air at 3:00 in the Morning

We have a woodstove at our house. Actually, it's a wood furnace. It's a big green metal box in the basement that pipes heat through the duct work. It takes up a lot of room, but that's okay. Our basement is concrete and unfinished and we mostly use it for storage. My husband spends time down there butchering deer and cleaning his guns and doing other manly things like organizing nails and screws. I don't go down there very often. Except in the fall and winter, when I have to feed the furnace.

Burning wood is great! First of all, it costs us nothing because my husband works for a tree service and we get the wood for free. Yay! He splits it and stacks it and we always have enough to last us through the cold months. And burning wood heats the house so well! Sometimes a little too well. When you get that furnace cranking, it really kicks out the heat. We have adjustable vents, but even when we close them it is sometimes too hot. Like really hot. Can you say fiery furnace? So, we open the windows. Yep, on any given day in winter, it may be twenty-two degrees outside, but you'll likely find the windows open at my house.

My favorite thing about burning wood is the smell. I adore the scent of wood smoke. It smells like home and comfort. It makes me feel warm and cozy. I wish I had wood smoke-scented perfume. Or a candle. That way I could enjoy it even in the heat of summer. It really is one of my favorite scents. Except one time, it wasn't.

One cold winter's night, I awoke to an odd smell. And when I say odd smell, I mean stinky smell. Really stinky. Putrid, even. I mean, it smelled so bad it woke me out of a peaceful sleep. I sat up in bed. I covered my nose. I tried to breathe through my mouth. I glanced at my husband. Surely, he could smell it, too. But no! He was still fast asleep. Snoring. Sawing logs. He must have been dreaming about chopping firewood. He looked so peaceful. It was annoying! I was tempted to pinch his nose shut until he woke up. But I didn't. I just shook him until he woke up and then asked if he could smell whatever that disgusting smell was. It took his brain a minute to connect with his nose, but when it finally did, he said he smelled something, too. But he couldn't identify it either. So we sat there, in the darkness, on the edge of the bed, in the wee hours of the morning, sniffing the air! We sniffed and sniffed. And then we gagged a little. But we just didn't know what we were sniffing! It smelled hot. Like something was burning. It may have been my nose hairs! I'm pretty sure that rank odor went right up my nostrils and singed them. Maybe I had a chemical burn.

We decided to investigate. As we stepped into the hall, the stench grew stronger. We walked into the living room, the dining room, and then the kitchen. With each step we took, the repulsive smell intensified. But we couldn't tell where it was coming from. We looked all over the house, like we were on some kind of bizarre treasure hunt. There was no smoke that we could see, so wie didn't think the house was on fire. It didn't smell electrical. The oven was turned off. I even walked over and sniffed the dog. She just smelled like her normal stink.

My husband decided the offensive odor must be coming from outside. Maybe the neighbors were burning something. At 3:00 in the morning. Right outside our bedroom window. Sure, that seemed likely. There was only one place left in the house to check. The basement. There was no way I was going down there in the dark with a mysterious stink creeping through the house. So I stayed put, holding my nose in the kitchen, while my brave husband went to investigate. He was gone for a long time. Like five minutes. Which seemed like a fairly long time to find an odor in a basement. But he found it! He found the source of the stink! And believe me when I say you will never guess what it was.

Dog poop! The wretched stink was burning dog poop!

Our dog had been in the basement earlier in the day. And she had pooped on the floor. And my husband cleaned it up, like any good husband would. But he made a fatal error. Instead of taking the poop outside to dispose of properly, he dropped it in the ash can! Yep, the ash trash can! The big metal trash can we use to dispose of ashes from the furnace. For some reason, my husband thought it would be a good idea to throw fresh dog poop into a can of ashes. That were still hot. The dog poop sat in the hot ashes for hours and hours, until it started to smolder. And that, my friends, is what woke me up at 3:00 in the morning. Burning dog poop! I had the smell of burning dog poop in my nostrils. Burning dog poop had singed my nose hairs! The stench of smoldering dog poop had seeped into every nook and cranny of my home. We would have to move. So, at 3:00 in the morning, my husband took out the ashes. And I opened a window!

Have you ever hidden dog poop in a can of burning ashes? I hope not! But have you ever tried to hide your sins? Maybe not in a trash can. But from your family? From yourself? Or even from God? Usually when we try to hide something, it's because we are ashamed. Or embarrassed. And we don't want anyone to know about it. But keeping things hidden only leads to trouble. It causes pain. And hurt. And eventually it starts to stink, and everyone around you can smell the odor.

We all sin. Every one of us. Romans 3:23 reminds us, "for all have sinned and fall short of the glory of God." But we do not have to hide that sin from God! In fact, we can't hide that sin from God, even if we try! God wants us to bring our sins to him. He is waiting with open arms. In 1 John 1:9, we read the promise, "If we confess our sins, he is faithful and just and will forgive us our sins and purify us from all unrighteousness."

No need to hide. Forgiveness awaits! Trying to hide your sin from God is pointless. It doesn't work. And eventually, it begins to stink!

Once you smell the stench of sin, it is a smell you will never want to smell again. Just like burning dog poop. Literally the stinkiest stink I've ever smelled!

It's time to take out the ashes!

PRAYER:

Dear Lord, sin stinks! I want it out of my life. Search
my heart and every hidden part of me so I can see what
I need to get rid of. Thank you for forgiving me.

Acknowledgements

Thank you, Lord, for giving me the love of writing, and the desire to encourage others by sharing my stories. Thank you for loving me, saving me, and showing up in my ordinary life!

Thanks to my family, who graciously allow me to tell stories about our lives!

To my handsome husband, who is my biggest supporter. He encourages me, cheers me on, holds me up, and nudges me when necessary!

To my two beautiful daughters, who are always willing to listen to my stories, and who give me so much to write about!

And to whoever may be reading this book, thank you for letting me share my words with you!

About the Author

Heidi Poe is a wife, mother, writer, storyteller, follower of Jesus, and lover of all things chocolate and peanut butter. Through her writing, she tells stories of her average, ordinary, everyday life, sprinkled with a healthy dose of sass, a wee bit of sarcasm, and a generous helping of Scripture. She hopes to encourage women to look for the ways God shows up in their everyday lives, and remind them that living an ordinary life is a beautiful thing!